Riding the Path to Healing

Jean T. Slobodzian

Published by Nine Bells Books, 2024.

RIDING THE PATH TO HEALING

First edition. July 22, 2024.

Copyright © 2024 Jean T. Slobodzian.

ISBN: 979-8990827509

Written by Jean T. Slobodzian.

Table of Contents

To Susan and Juan, whose ministry of good deeds at their equine therapy ranch has inspired this fictional tale.

Adjusting the Lens

Allow me to introduce myself. I am formally known as Thou-Est but am called by many other names and titles, among them Guardian, Angel and Spirit. I happily answer to any and all who call upon me by whatever name they wish.

Those of us who have been chosen, including the ones who have already come and the ones who have yet to arrive, all begin in the same way—by first drifting, seemingly aimlessly but actually purposefully, throughout the Universe. There is indeed a solid and important reason for this time of drifting, for each chosen one must be trained during the journey to reach a place of understanding, not just in the general ways of the cosmos but also in the specific manner in which we are to conduct ourselves once we reach the final important and critical destination for which we were originally chosen. No matter how fast or slow our progress, we are all reminded, again and again, that the path to understanding will be different for every one of us and that, instead of looking at each other to compare and evaluate our own rate of learning, we should instead look inward, rejoicing in our own unique nature.

I tried my best not to look to others to determine how I measured up, but I couldn't help but see that my time of drifting literally lasted far longer than most of the others who were chosen. My time of drifting lasted for eons. So, I guess I was what could be called a slow learner. But at least I was learning. I tried my best to glean something from each and every single thing I experienced. And it wasn't just that I needed more time, but I could see that I was different in several other ways. I have a tendency to wander all about while recounting events and am often

1

told to stick to the point (I try very hard to remind myself when I go too far afield in my sharing of incidents) and I also have a deep-seated habit of repeating information over and over until it finally becomes ingrained in my very psyche.

Yes, it has taken me many experiences and much time to finally grasp that no two of us are alike. Once I truly understood that, then I began to feel deep inside of me that the differences are what make us all beautiful and glorious. Because I've come to this way of thinking, I usually feel at peace and have come to grips with who I am, but back then I spent too much time noticing and worrying about the quality of my aptitudes and abilities. It was during those occasions when I began to doubt exactly what my personal path was to be or even wonder if my skill set would allow me to be successful on that path, I would stop and say to myself that learning would come and once it did, my ultimate purpose would then be revealed and that I had to have faith in my own abilities. The important thing, I told myself at these times of uncertainty, was the process that guided me toward the product of the final desired result. And once I finally accepted that reasoning, I would be left without further thought or worry as I would thankfully never have to compare myself any more to the others who had been chosen. Bit by bit, I came to see that each one of us would all arrive at the place of understanding, and by doing so, we would each reach our maximum potential so that we could then support and serve needs greater than our own. And that self-talk would calm me down, at least during the particular moment of hesitation I was feeling.

Time passes in its own way for those who have been chosen, so I cannot explain exactly how long my process of developing was taking. All I know is that I was continually kept busy, usually assigned various minor tasks that would help tend to the needs of given stars and planets through each of their life cycles. Once in a great while, I helped manage galactic orbs as they first formed but more often was called upon to nurse them through their final stages of existence, guiding them through their cycle of existence until they gradually became so old that they would disintegrate and finally disappear.

I was captivated by each of my assignments and found dealing with these relatively "lifeless" spatial entities interesting, but I never realized the immense appeal being around life forms would hold until I was assigned to the second largest galaxy of the local group, the Virgo Supercluster of galaxies, for contained within this gravity-bound entity was an even smaller galaxy that had always drawn my attention, the one which is known by many different names, such as: the Badurru, the Silver River, the Backbone of the Night and the Milky Way. But none of those names do it justice or describe all the beauty and mystery that abounds, for within this vast setting is one particular planet that over time pulled me in, not only literally by its own gravitational force (which was quite strong) but by the appearance of something I had never before encountered.

Humans.

People.

So seemingly simple a life-form but actually so completely and utterly complex.

Once assigned to this planet that is known as Earth, I was first expected to become familiar with all the things about this very unique place. I studied the locations and properties of the many fresh, brackish and salt bodies of water, the environments and survival habits of each and every animal species, the wide variety of flowers and trees both growing in the wild and being cultivated, and of course, was directed to pay extra close attention to the customs and behaviors of that most special animal: humans. I spent centuries just floating among, above, below, and within the wide number of people living all around the globe. My task was to observe them up close so I could take note of their individual characteristics and also to watch them from afar so I could learn how they evolved from very primitive beings to highly sophisticated users of the resources available to them.

I studied the revolutions and rotations of this planet, the power of the rising and setting of the sun, the spreading and receding of glaciers, the creation of the seas, the influence of the moon upon the tides, the ever-changing weather conditions that continually force adaptations on all living creatures, the stars that guide wanderers on their treks, and the fluctuating of the seasons both in the Northern and Southern Hemispheres.

And in all that while, of course, a great deal of time passed. My one job during that whole phase of my assignment was to watch and only to watch. I was under strict instructions to observe and learn, but never to interfere nor intercede. I came to see that communication among living beings is crucial to their survival, so I learned the various languages both spoken and signed by different groups of people inhabiting every land mass around this planet. I made it a goal to keep current with changes taking place in the different groups as they each evolved over time. In addition, I became fluent in the languages of all animal species and also tuned into the ways that plants communicate with one another.

I was told that all this learning was essential because it would assist me upon the appointed and predetermined hour when my true calling was revealed. Because I was not given any hint as to what my true calling would be, I made every effort to stay open to all that was happening before me. Things that I saw early on might become important later. How was I to know what would make the difference to my success or failure once I knew what my mission would be? I didn't. And I knew that I needed to take it all in, not only recognizing what I was observing but then also analyzing it, as well. At different points along the way during this protracted period of time I sometimes became frustrated and overwhelmed. But I knew I couldn't give up. The only way I managed to keep going was by stepping back and taking some time to reflect upon what I was experiencing and by digging deep within myself to where I would ultimately find a level of unbounded patience and unshakable faith that I had hitherto not even known existed within me. Once I found that faith, I was not only able to go on, but was eager to do so and because of that renewed strength, my focus on observation and analysis of what I was witnessing increased exponentially and thus, my level of learning also increased. I no longer worried about how long it was taking me to soak in all that was before me but instead I was able to hone in on what I was learning. What I came to understand was that as soon as I began to make a few connections it became easier to make more and more.

Sure enough, finally on a given day in a given year, the miracle occurred. I was sent up into the heavens to sit at the knee of The One Who Guides Us All. There I was told that my time of drifting, observing, and learning was ending. I was informed that I was being appointed to serve as an Earth-Bound Attendant. I liked the sound of that title but wondered what it really meant. The One Who Guides Us All explained that the ultimate goal of this assignment would be to pave the way so that kindness and love were allowed to thrive. I rejoiced at that moment because after spending so much time travelling all around Earth, it was clear to me that things were always made better when kindness and love were present.

I was ready to rush back to my planet-home because I knew that all I had to do was spread the word near and far, quickly and loudly in order to show everyone there the way they should live. I couldn't help but think about how easy it was going to be to bring about positive change. This was the best task I could have imagined and I turned to say my thanks for such a wonderful assignment but before I could utter a word, I was stopped in my tracks, for The One already knew what was on my mind. And it was then that I learned about the specific parameters to this assignment that would prohibit me from preaching and that I was under strict instructions to never overtly step in or take direct control of any events. Before I had time to share one single complaint or worry, The One went on to tell me what I was allowed to do, which was to offer support, suggestions, and guidance from afar. To put it out there into the ether, so to speak, and to wait to see if my ideas got noticed and if they did, perhaps they would be accepted. I began to see the value in this approach and came to envision that if all that happened then surely a positive difference was not only possible but inevitable.

I went back to my planet-home to begin this most sacred of assignments and over the years as an Earth-Bound Attendant, my presence has indeed not only blessedly and positively impacted the existence of plants and animals, but most especially has helped those who have the greatest influence on the health of this big blue globe called Earth, which is humanity in general and more specifically, has strengthened and improved the existence of a select number of children and adults residing on all the different continents, living in diverse ways from one another.

What I have come to see is that, unlike all the other animals and all the plants, humans are truly unique. Observing them over many years I have observed that this special status is borne out in ways that, even to this day, I am still struggling to grasp. While humans are the most dominant force on this planet, sometimes they seem to take this status for granted, neither harnessing the potential that their combined power would have to raise up the status of all its citizens nor to serve as caretakers for the health of the planet itself. It baffles me why people use a lot of their time and energy comparing and contrasting how their outward appearances as well as their inner belief systems are different from each other and instead of rejoicing in those dissimilarities, they tend to view them in a way that doesn't make the larger group stronger but somehow weakens the whole of humanity. They purposefully divide into all kinds of categories by separating themselves based on pre-constructed racial, religious, geographical, and gender groupings. What they can't seem to see is that these groupings have the opposite effect of bringing them together and often leaves them hopelessly set apart from one another.

I have incorporated many strategies to help people come together. If they could only grasp the power of the knowledge that has been made available through scientific discovery, which is supported and sponsored by The One Who Guides Us All. Then they would see such seemingly obvious differences of skin color, height, weight, and gender are actually superficial alterations of a basic inner core. I thought the matter would be settled once the discovery was made showing that the physical bodies of all humans are truly more similar than dissimilar, once the discovery that all bodies have those two long, twisted strands containing the genetic blueprint for individuals known as the biomolecule called deoxyribonucleic acid (DNA). Instead of perseverating on external physical differences, if people just instead looked deeper, and consider that DNA is actually 99.9% alike between and among each one of them, they would come to realize that all those who are of the species Homo sapiens have more in common than not. If only they could focus less on their outer shells and more on their minds, hearts and souls they would come to see that there are things they all share, and not the least among them is the need to love and be loved.

Oh my, that's just one example of how I have tried to figure out why there is such a disconnect between what is known with what is seen. The overall disparity between groups of people often overtakes my understandings of the world at large but then I am reminded by the powers that be to step back and focus on both the macro and the micro views of what is happening all over this planet lovingly nicknamed The Big Blue Marble. The kindnesses I have seen, the love that is being spread, the positive changes I have witnessed happening when goodness is shared between two or more individual people. In the end, perhaps, the macro and micro perspectives balance out, for I have been privy to so many positive life affirming events in my time here on Earth.

The stories I could tell!

But, one caveat for this particular assignment of mine is that those stories must be confidentially held and not shared. At least, not shared until the time is right. That determination is not of my own making, but comes from The One Who Guides Us All and thus must be obeyed. There will come a day when I will be allowed and encouraged to regale you with the wide width and breadth of my experiences, even those that occurred long ago in human history, and believe me they are all still fresh in my mind. But the telling of those ancient pre-historic and historic tales and even most of the events I have witnessed more recently is not to be ... not yet. With one glorious exception.

As I said, I've been around this planet for quite a while and had come to the point where I thought I had seen it all. However, a few years ago (Earth time) I was given a new assignment and I quickly figured out that I still had more to learn about the ways and means of humans when they truly wanted to do well by and for each other. I understood that this would serve as an elevation in my career path because it required an increase of responsibility on my part and that there would now be a new focus that entailed a vital and important mission for me, as I was charged with watching over one specific location where several humans had intentionally gathered together for a common purpose.

To begin this assignment, I was given time to observe so I could develop an understanding of the circumstances that brought together these individuals. What was made clear to me from the outset was that these people were true and righteous believers of all that is seen and unseen, and most especially of The One Who Guides Us All—whom they knew and referred to as the trinity of Father, Son, and Holy Spirit. It also quickly became obvious that they looked at their fellow humans in an opposite way than most people tend to do, seeing each other kind of "inside out" so to speak. What I mean by that is, whenever they would meet a new person, they automatically looked beyond the physical shell and instead focused on the glow of humanity that was emanating outward from that person.

What an amazing thing that was to behold! And not only did they see people differently, they also treated those people more lovingly and respectfully, as well. From my first day on this particular job to this very day, I have witnessed these humans to whom I am currently attached consistently display such kind, loving attitudes that neither time nor circumstance have altered as they continue to honor the Universe by treating all flora, fauna, and fellow humans equally, and even more significant than that, fairly.

As soon as I began this current assignment, I knew it was going to be special in multiple ways. So, for the first time ever, I sought permission from The One to allow me to tell the tales of living and working alongside Sally and Mateo at The Palm Tree Ranch located in San Carlos, which is in the Sonoran region of Mexico.

Amazingly, The One approved my request! I received permission to tell the story of those whom I currently shadow. Thus, their adventures have been written down and are now being shared with you, my dear Gentle Readers.

On the surface, it may seem that I am simply describing everyday, ordinary life on the Ranch. However, I hope that as you dig deeper down in this story, you will be able to see the power of unending and abiding love that those involved have for a Higher Being. If so, you will surely marvel as you see how strong love and everlasting faith can manifest itself in the respect that is shown for life itself, in all forms.

In this recounting, I shall serve as Docent while we tour and get to know the comings and goings of those on The Ranch. Be prepared to learn about traditionally under or never represented lives, for their stories shall become available to you in this text either through their own voices or through my telling of the tales.

As the anecdotes channel through me, I will be changing all names and altering some identifying details so that the right to privacy for those involved, who are still living and making their way through this world even to today, will be honored and respected. My hope is that you will come to appreciate that those minor details really do not matter as much as the overall message that is being told. If you give these stories a chance, the power of the good work being done at The Palm Tree Ranch will surely shine through and Heavens-Above willing, might touch your hearts, perhaps providing balm for any needed healing in your own lives. And maybe, just maybe, inspire you to look from a similar perspective as those of our main characters in this story, which in turn very well might positively alter the impact you have upon this world.

In this book, there will first be a description of the two critically important humans: Sally and Mateo. After that you will meet the herd of horses living on The Ranch. As you will come to learn, each one found its way to this destination differently. All were meant to be here and all are now set free of worry and woe, for the mission of healing others could not be completed without first offering comfort and healing to those who are destined to do the work. After I focus on the story of Sally and Mateo, and then after those four horses separately are given the opportunity to introduce themselves, I will return and share with you a few stories of how equine therapy is used with children by providing a few case studies. I'm praying that my tale will help you to see what can be accomplished when humans (and horses, too!) take action to help others and the amazing strength of character that comes of being guided and supported by their personal interpretations of Divine Intervention. When you have finished reading about life on The Palm Tree Ranch, I hope that you come to not only recognize but to deeply respect the strength and power of love, which always changes everyone and everything for the better.

Call and Response

T he reason I have spent many centuries drifting from place to place
around this planet Earth is because I've been assigned to shadow
quite a wide array of people in a wide variety of locations. In all that
time, I have come to witness daily life interactions between different
people on every spot of land considered at all habitable by humans.

There I was, floating around and above this planet as cavemen
shifted from foraging in the woods for their food to becoming
hunter-gatherers and then watching as people moved on to become
farmers and consumers.

Evolution of all kinds took place during this timeframe. As the
planet itself changed, with glaciers receding, volcanoes erupting, land
forms shifting, all manner of plants and animals came and went, some
surviving while others became extinct, with human adaptation varying
in specific and noticeable ways from that of all other living creatures.

Not only did people begin to set traps and use tools for acquiring
food and clothing materials and not only did they begin to create
sophisticated dwellings to protect themselves from the elements and
other animals of prey, but probably most importantly, they developed
what linguists label "protolanguages" (and yes, even though never
documented nor specifically analyzed, take it from me that such
precursors existed and helped form the many and assorted languages
used around the world today). I have witnessed first-hand the manner
in which people of long-ago developed methods for communicating
with one another, first somewhat indirectly by using cave paintings,
then more directly by pointing, grunting, speaking and signing to get

their messages across, and currently to modern times where not only do they share ideas in person or through the airwaves, but where writing has been enhanced to such a degree that it includes both words as well as images. Over all this time, even with the seemingly intense and rapid evolution of communication methods, there always seemed to be one shared goal: to provide a forum for people to convey their thoughts and feelings.

Let me tell you, all the Heavens rejoiced when humans first began to create beautifully sophisticated versions of both spoken and signed languages, and those up above continue to rejoice to this very day, as there are now almost 7,500 documented unique languages used by humans all around the world!

Yes, the Heavens may have rejoiced, but at the same time, those who watch over the Universe also grieved, for they saw that despite all these wondrous gifts of thinking, inventing, creating, traveling, and most especially of the use of sophisticated languages that only humans possess, instead of driving people towards one another rejoicing in their blessed humanity, these things have actually served to drive them apart from each other.

Those who are wiser than me keep faith and hope that perhaps at some point in the future people may come to understand that each and every language should be treasured for its own complexities and to respect and delight in the shared abilities and wisdom that helped to create so many different communication systems, but as it stands now, when people from two distinct cultural groups or geographical areas meet, they often focus on the surface differences (such as the way they dress or the foods they eat) and not on the deep-rooted commonalities between their lives (such as the need for shelter, feelings of safety and devotion to loved ones).

While it might seem natural that different languages, on the surface, would serve to divide people, the fact is that every language used in this whole wide world shares one important requirement: it must contain an agreed-upon set of grammatical rules.

Words or signs are made from smaller parts that join together in specific ways to create those larger parts. Any and every thing that can be thought can be expressed through language. All languages are "living" entities, which means that each language must continually meet the needs of those in the cultural community who rely on it for communicating their ideas, concerns, feelings and experiences.

Interestingly, languages are not static, which means that for any individual language to survive it must inevitably change over time to adapt and meet the needs of those currently using it for communication purposes. Knowing that some languages from long ago are no longer used at all and are considered "dead" to the world should impress upon people the fragility of something that on the surface seems so strong, but instead most people—then and now—ignore the bigger picture. Sadly, humans have always worked desperately to obtain and maintain a falsely constructed hierarchy of status. They play the "us against them" game which time and time again has only yielded division and destruction.

Now, you have to understand that I am not privileged to see the entire grand plan designed by The One Who Guides Us All, so I really can't grasp why different people segregate themselves around this planet in the ways that they do and why one of those factors rests upon the belief that their particular language is better or more important than the language used by another group of people. Ah well, someday I may comprehend it all. But for now, I need to use my own current language of choice and get back to writing the story I was authorized to tell, for I have clearly wandered a bit far afield.

So, yes, let us return to the tale of The Palm Tree Ranch ... and to do that we need to begin by looking at two important locations on this globe:

Beverly, Massachusetts, United States of America.

Heroica Veracruz, Mexico.

Our two human heroes of this story, Sally and Mateo, were born and grew up, respectively, in those two localities. Anyone who knew either Sally or Mateo as children would surely never have been able to predict that their individual life-paths would lead them to eventually come together where they would share not only a working relationship but a loving one, as well. Yet, here they are.

While both of their childhood towns are located in the eastern portion of their respective countries and both are on the continent of North America, you might assume they are relatively near to one another but in actuality they are quite a long distance apart. Not only were these two young people separated by a vast geographical expanse, but also by the cultures of their people and by the languages they spoke. Sally's first language was English; it was only as an adult, when she graduated from college with a bachelor's degree and opted to move to New Mexico so she could further her education by obtaining her doctorate as a physical therapist that she found she had an affinity for learning languages and rapidly becoming fluent in reading, writing and speaking Spanish. As for Mateo, although his native language was Spanish, he learned English quickly and efficiently in grade school and then at a much more sophisticated level while in high school. His near-native knowledge of English served him well when he moved to New Mexico to attend college on a sports scholarship, playing on the soccer team. During this time, he not only studied accounting but also met Sally, who by then was hired as a pediatric physical therapist for a local clinic.

Their first meeting happened early on in the soccer season, when one of the players on the team twisted his ankle during a home game. Sally was there to watch the game and noticed that the team doctor, who happened to be her friend, was busy with another player at the time, so she came down out of the stands and offered to tend to the ankle injury. Despite the player's declaration that he was feeling okay,

Sally evaluated the situation, saw the rapid swelling of the foot and determined that the ankle was surely sprained. She told the player that it would need immediate attention so it did not become worse. Before the player could argue any more, one of his teammates walked over to where they were sitting on the end of the bench, sat down and calmly recounted a story of how the same thing happened to a different teammate during a game played when he was in high school. That young boy ignored doctor's advice, ran back out to join in the action, couldn't support his weight and twisted that same ankle again, falling down before play could even resume. Unable to stand up and walk on his own, he had to be carried off the field on a stretcher. Turned out that his entire season was over and he never could play soccer again with the same carefree abandon as he had before that injury. Sally noticed that this story calmed down the injured player and he agreed to sit out the rest of the game. The team doctor, who by this time had finished taking care of the other player, came over to the bench and Sally was free to go. She smiled as she headed back to the stands. She knew immediately that there was something special about that man who calmed down the injured player.

Sally waited after the game was over so she could check in with her friend, the team doctor. He told her that thanks to her quick response in elevating and icing the ankle, the injury would only require a short time to heal. While they were chatting, the other player came back out onto the field and introduced himself to Sally. And that was how Sally and Mateo met. They began dating but shortly afterwards Sally was offered a new job in a different state. She took that job and sadly, Sally and Mateo drifted apart. Mateo graduated and became an accountant for a firm located near the college he had attended. Sally's career thrived in that town in Colorado, so far away from where Mateo lived in New Mexico.

It wasn't long before they each found a partner, each got married and each had children with their respective spouses. Sadly, neither marriage worked out and within a decade, there were two divorces. Mateo stayed in the same town where he had been married so he could share custody of their daughter with his ex-wife. Sally found herself living a single mother's life in Colorado, as her ex-husband decided he was not meant for married life and one day, while Sally was at work and the children were at school, he just packed up his clothes and deserted his family. Leaving behind a hastily written note on the kitchen counter, he walked out of the door and moved to parts unknown as quickly as he could. His truly selfish nature willed out and as soon as he decided that he wanted nothing more to do with Sally, his son or his daughter, he never looked back.

The dissolution of her marriage took its toll and Sally was overwhelmed with all the responsibility that had been thrust upon her shoulders so quickly. She felt lost and alone, but each day she prayed for guidance, believing that one way or another it would be possible to overcome this unforeseen calamity. The children were in pain, as well, and many long nights were spent with the three of them talking about their feelings and reviewing their options. Months went by and as the reality of now being a family of three sank in, they all agreed that change might be a good thing.

One evening, Sally posed the possibility of finding a new place where they could have a fresh start and go forward in life instead of feeling too closely tied to their painful past. Without hesitation, both of her children grabbed onto that idea and at the end of the school year, they moved out of their house, which had sold quickly after being put on the market.

As they packed up all their belongings, not one of the three of them regretted the decision and instead of looking back at all they were leaving, were looking forward to where they were going and all the possibilities that lied ahead.

Ironically, the place they chose together was not just a step forward into the future but also a step back into the past for Sally. Having heard stories of the courage and strength it took when she made her first big move away from her childhood home in Massachusetts so many years ago, the children pushed to move to a new state. Well, at least a new state for the two young ones, as they all chose to return to the town in New Mexico where Sally had first landed as an adult, for they knew how happy she had been there so many years ago. Instead of buying a house, they decided to rent an apartment, just in case this really wasn't the best location for them, but it quickly became clear that they had made a good decision, for it seemed to take no time at all before the children had easily and happily made the adjustment to their new location, finding friends in the neighborhood and in their new school.

Amazingly, once there, Sally found Mateo again. Their love for each other was as strong as it was when they were young people and the two of them knew at once they were being given a second chance. It wasn't long before they grabbed that chance and, with the blessings of their own three children, married and became a true and forever blended family. Happily, there has been no looking back and it is clear not only to them but to everyone who meets them, that they were destined to be together.

The friendship that quickly developed to love was then lost by the couple who drifted apart and then replaced once more, this time to be melded back together even stronger than it had been the first time. They embraced each other's children and those feelings of love were directed right back at them. Being a couple once again was even sweeter and easier than ever. In no small part, it helped that the two of them had so much in common. Yes, it was wonderful that they found enjoyment from many of the same recreational and social activities such as reading, going to the theatre, taking outdoor hikes, but it was even more wonderful that they were each filled with the need to reach out beyond their own lives to serve the needs of others. Above and beyond all that, the glue which held them together and the most important belief both of them held was a deep and abiding faith that they were being guided by a higher power. The shared gift they have of seeing beyond the superficial characteristics of the body directly into the heart and soul of each person they meet allows them to accept others without judgement. Of course, though it probably does not need saying, let me say it never occurred to either Sally or Mateo that language, geographical location or culture of birth should keep them apart.

Destiny meant for them to find each other and to be together. Their love has only grown stronger and more secure over all these years. They are not only both bilingual, but have become bicultural, and very much devoted to each other. Their journey to sharing life together has not always been easy or smooth for either of them, but what a miracle that after they had each began to raise their individual families, lost their original partners and were left feeling lonely and somewhat at a loss, they met once more and this time fell deeply and permanently in love.

Now, their lives are meshed together and they have successfully blended those two originally separate familial groups into one strong and loving unit. These days, they have three biological children between them who are now grown and out on their own. The home Sally and Mateo created at The Pine Tree Ranch turns out to be not only large enough to house the two of them but has enough room for visits from their own dear children and their children's children and also offers shelter for any and all of the foster children who are periodically placed under their protective care.

To look at Sally, who is a petite and slim woman well into middle age, you would not expect the strength she can summon when helping to lift a child up onto a horse or when throwing hay to feed the horses. And her college degree in physical therapy certainly serves her well, for she is skilled in evaluating and applying rehabilitative treatment programs for each individual child-in-need who arrives at The Ranch. Top that off with her deep understanding of hippotherapy and how horses can help improve the physical health of humans in need and you have a winning combination.

Mateo, also in his middle years here on the planet, offers a bit more of a commanding first impression than his partner. Standing at least a foot taller than Sally, posture straight and confident, Mateo quickly instills a feeling of calm in all those who are in his presence. Ignoring the fact that there is not a hair on his head, one is instead drawn to the constant and radiant smile always present on his face. In addition to the business and accounting expertise that he brings to the workings at The Ranch, he also has the muscles needed for the very physically demanding work that takes place each and every day.

Like most true heroes, our two main human characters in this story, Sally and Mateo, are reserved in their use of self-praise. While they spend a great deal of time reflecting on how best to serve their community and the needs of all the children brought to The Ranch for therapy, those who are medically fragile, emotionally needy, or who have been diagnosed as disabled, they spend very little time reflecting on the wonderful gift that they, themselves, are offering all those who cross their paths.

Their lives are designed in a most pragmatic fashion. They focus on logistics as they figure out how to manage the workload needed to accomplish their day-to-day tasks, first and foremost keeping an eye on staying true to their overall mission. And whenever they are asked about their own roles or whenever they are given compliments and praise, they take very little credit, instead offering up all honor and glory to The One (whom Sally and Mateo know as the triune God—the trinity of the Father, the Son Jesus and the Holy Spirit).

Sally and Mateo are confident that the work they are doing at The Pine Tree Ranch is, in many ways, not of their choosing but instead is their destiny. More than two decades ago, they looked around and saw pain and sorrow where there should have been only joy. I have often heard them explain to others about why they are walking down this professional and personal life path of providing equine therapy to young people in need, "Our Bible tells us that we are each perfectly and wonderfully made. With that in mind, it's hard to imagine why God would have selected some children to suffer and struggle in ways that most children do not. But we look at it differently. Instead of thinking that any child's life is a mistake, we prefer to change the conception of what the terms perfect and wonderful mean, because we honestly believe that we were all put here on Earth purposefully and that God doesn't make mistakes. Therefore, we are all perfect and wonderful in our own way."

Not content to let it rest with that declaration, they tend to go on by explaining, "And all children, whether strong or medically fragile, are deserving of our love, but most especially those children who endured emotional or physical trauma during their young lives are certainly deserving not only of our love but also of our assistance. It's up to us to accept and care for every child the best we can. When we can reach out and support young children in need, not only are their lives changed for the better but ours is also changed as well, for we become stronger, more patient, more thankful people."

They aren't just spouting platitudes or trying to get you to think they are saints here on Earth. Sally and Mateo both talk-the-talk and walk-the-walk. Once the switch for them was made from working what is known as regular day jobs to answering the call to service that they heard from The One Who Guides Us All, the one they call God, the path to creating and sustaining The Palm Tree Ranch was firmly underway and there was no going back to that old way of life, nor was there any desire on their part to do so. None of it came easily, but obstacles never did deter them, as you will now learn through the tale of how The Ranch came to fruition. What a joyful time it has been to behold them as they followed the path they so clearly imagined together, first designing and then working, step by step, to change their vision from dream to reality.

A Mission to Serve

S o many in this world are suffering, and so much needs to be done to bring them out of their pain-filled states. Occasionally the solution seems obvious but more often than not it is difficult to discern exactly how to offer support. Some people feel overwhelmed by the needs of others and either give up entirely or perhaps even worse, try to determine who is most worthy of attention and who can be ignored. Among the many things I have learned from The One Who Guides Us All is that it is not the responsibility of humans to determine why things exist on this planet, but it is incumbent upon them to accept and honor the idea that everything has been created on purpose and with a purpose. From the smallest speck of dust or grain of sand to the largest whale or redwood tree, from the things that might seem irritating to people and animals alike all the way to the easily agreed upon most wondrous creatures, there should be rejoicing and appreciation that the gift of life has been given to each and every single one. Focus should be not only on self-protection, but also on protecting everything that exists here on Earth.

This is just my personal opinion, and I'm not taking away from the hardships endured by any other animals or plants who inhabit this planet, but I believe that people might have the hardest task of all when it comes to the area of caring for both themselves and for others. Humans are the most intellectual, most developed, and most interactive beings out of everything and everyone living here on Earth. They think and they share their thoughts. They feel emotions and they share those feelings. They invent and they share those creations. You get the gist. In a nutshell, humans have been given wide-ranging and powerful gifts that others have not and they use those gifts in a variety of ways. But, over the years, the development of those gifts has actually created quite a quandary.

Here on Earth, I have often heard people repeat two well-known sayings in various situations and I believe that they might help to explain the dilemma which exists between being given, possessing, and utilizing such gifts. The first saying is: "With great power comes great responsibility" which means that if you have both the ability and opportunity to do something, you should do it for the good of everyone. The second is: "To whom much is given, much will be required" which means that any particular talents, skills, knowledge, or wealth that you possess should be used for the betterment of not only yourself, but of others, as well.

Some people easily understand that they should give back to others and that when they support their peers, everyone succeeds. However, there is also another group of people who take the opposing view and believe that there is only room for good things to happen in their own lives and that anyone else who tries to succeed shouldn't get the chance because, somehow or other, in their own minds they don't believe those people are deserving of success.

I try to resolve these contradictory reactions that humans have toward themselves and others, but find myself never coming up with a clear understanding of it all. Whenever I get the chance, I question those working in positions higher than mine, asking for clarification about why some humans squander the opportunity to help spread the wealth, so as to ensure that all share in the glories that they themselves have been given. Each time, I inevitably receive a response that, in human culture, would be comparable to a pat on the head and a sigh.

"Oh, Thou-Est," those who watch from above usually begin their response, and then always say almost the very same thing to me, "humans are the most complex entity ever created. Even more complicated than the solar system itself! They, and they alone, have the greatest gift, which is the ability to reason and to reflect upon their options."

At which point I tend to interrupt and ask, over and over again in all these multiple conversations, "If they can choose goodness and light, why then do I witness so much hatred? So much alienation? Such loneliness and despair?"

And the response always follows these same lines, "Because humans think too much."

"What does that mean?"

"Well," the patient and guiding ones then say, "if they learned to listen to their hearts and their souls, the path would be easy. It would be to follow what over time has come to be known as The Golden Rule: to treat others as you would wish to be treated."

"But that seems too easy, too simple," I will usually complain.

"Yes, easy and simple, Thou-Est. It is not a new concept, as it has been viewed as a way to live since the dawn of time and has crossed continents, religions, and cultures. The reality is that this one idea, this one guiding principle, is all that is actually needed in the whole wide world. But far too often people stray from this ethical mantra more than they stay true to it. And that is why, although it seems easy and simple to us watchers, it is actually so difficult and complex at the same time for those who are living on Earth."

Usually by now, I get overwhelmed with frustration at the whole human race and ask for a transfer of assignment. That is when The One Who Guides Us All intervenes and reminds me that my skills and talents are being put to their best use, encouraging me with the notion that I might be the one who helps to change the minds of many people, or just as importantly, if even one other person makes the shift from being selfish and uncaring to being compassionate and altruistic, that means my mission is succeeding.

Oh, and wouldn't I love to change the minds of people! I know I could do it in the blink of an eye, but I have been given very strict instructions on how I am allowed to interact with anyone or anything on Earth and I certainly cannot interfere with any decisions that humans make. I am, however, permitted to send out constant and unfaltering affirmatory dynamism and am also able to provide insight into all the options possible in every particular instance. I am meant to serve as a sort of conscience for those ready and willing to receive my message. But, and this is the most important but, it is up to each person to decide that it is time to share some of the blessings that have been bestowed upon them and to determine the best venue where their gifts and talents will do the most good.

Remembering that, I once again vow not to overthink my assignment and try to remember that because I am only allowed to widen the view and open the vision of possibilities, the ultimate decision on what to do with that new information is always left entirely up to the person with whom I am interacting. Somehow, hearing The One say this once more nourishes me and renews my resolve to return to Earth so I can again float above, between, under, and around all that is alive and use my energy to spread positivity to those with whom I come into contact.

Oh dear, I'm afraid I headed off on one of my tangents again, so I'd best stop digressing and return the focus once again to my most recent assignment, The Palm Tree Ranch, where I see the better side of the coin of human behavior in action and my spirits are always lifted by the unselfish, unwavering love and support offered to those in need by all who live and work there. When I first learned all about Sally and Mateo, the two people who established The Ranch, I began to feel a strong desire to tell their story because the work they have done has brought about much positive change to many around them.

The primary mission of The Palm Tree Ranch has not shifted since its inception, though it has grown in scope over the years. Children living with sorrowful feelings and broken hearts caused from childhood trauma, abuse, neglect or domestic violence are offered assistance, families desperate for information are offered support, and the whole greater community who often only experience frustration when they focus on negatives are provided real-life examples of what kindness and caring can look like and all the good that can flow from loving attention.

The original population of children receiving therapy at The Ranch were medically fragile, but at some point, Sally and Mateo became aware of yet another group of young people who were often neglected and generally underserved. Sally recognized that her professional therapeutic background would allow them to branch out in the services they offered and so they decided it was time to include another new direction that would focus on those children who are categorized as neurodivergent, meaning children who have been diagnosed as having autism spectrum disorder, attention-deficit hyperactivity disorder, or Down syndrome. More often than not, many of these of children arrive angry, upset and distrusting. No matter their background or circumstances, it seems that one thing they have in common is that, while they might completely shut down for a while, more times than not there are occasions when they become openly violent and disruptive. Mind you, this doesn't mean that these children are evil or even want to hurt other people, but instead this lashing out is primarily caused when they attempt to find a way to vent their inner frustrations of not having the necessary skills to communicate their thoughts, needs and desires. And because they tend not to have control over their own emotions or even their physical selves, it becomes near impossible to be able to avoid harming either themselves or others, and often times, both. Sally and Mateo used many strategies to enable the children to overcome their afflictions, but the greatest and most powerful tool they have is equine therapy.

In Sally's own words: "Over and over, time and time again, we have witnessed children who arrive here seemingly broken begin to blossom and grow. The trouble makers become peace makers. Those who could not hold themselves up when placed in a chair are able to independently sit up on a saddle while the horse beneath them slowly walks around the paddock. The greatest miracle of all is that whether they come from a home with supportive family members, from a house where their parents are no longer willing or able to take care of them, or from the local orphanage, once they begin to make progress, there's no holding them back."

Of course, riding on a horse does indeed provide therapeutic results, but it is not a panacea. Especially for those children who have been robbed of their innocence at a very young age, negative effects can be dramatic and devastating and will surely take a lifetime to heal. Continued and on-going therapy of various kinds is required in each and every one of those instances. But The Palm Tree Ranch is always a place where you can start to believe that positive change is possible.

Just so you don't get the mistaken idea that the groundwork that led to all the subsequent success in supporting the needs of the children happened in one day, one week, or even one month, let me be clear. It was a relatively long process that took a good deal of time to plan and organize. It wasn't just a matter of acquiring horses, but first there were also all the necessary preparations of the physical grounds that had to take place so they could be housed in a comfortable and nurturing environment. Once chosen and appropriately trained, the horses were then able to help make the dream Sally and Mateo had for the mission of The Ranch to come true.

So much to be done. Sally and Mateo were well aware of how many people living nearby were watching their progress and were waiting to utilize the therapy services they were planning to offer. Not only did neighbors often show up unannounced, just to say hello and see how things were coming along, but doctors at the local pediatric clinic kept calling at regular intervals to try to get a target date for the grand opening of The Ranch, always mentioning that they had several children already lined up as perfect candidates for such an innovative therapy option as was about to be offered. Sally and Mateo well knew the positive impact that equine therapy could provide for the members of their community. They understood the great need that was out there and worked tirelessly to get The Palm Tree Ranch up and running. But it wasn't easy for them.

As I've said before, all this did not happen overnight. For quite a while, they had a strong desire to embark on a new path in their shared life, but it was only a vague notion at that time. Back then, they were living in a traditional single-family dwelling in a suburban neighborhood, heading out to their individual 9-5 jobs each weekday, coming home each evening in time for dinner and getting to spend a few hours together before heading to bed to get rested so they could start it all over again the next morning. They were living in the moment, but always feeling something more awaited them. Mateo and Sally shared a deep rooted, faith-filled belief in the unlimited powers of wisdom, insight and counsel that are nurtured from connections with the heavens above. Strongly religious, they would pray together every day. Their prayers were always designed to honor and connect with their own God and to send the request that their lives be made useful and purposeful, in whatever fashion it was deemed best.

Now, the One Who Guides Us All did indeed hear the prayers of Sally and Mateo. In fact, The One tunes into all faithful believers, no matter what name they use when praying or in what specific fashion they worship. As long as the intent of their prayers comes from the goodness and kindness of their hearts and souls, The One will accept the message being sent. Sensing that Sally and Mateo were truly ready to make personal changes that could completely impact their work and their lives in general, The One determined it was time to offer them support as they began to make their yet unformed dreams come true.

It was at that very moment that I was chosen to walk in their combined shadow.

My orders were to never directly interfere with either Sally or Mateo as they embarked on their journey of discovery and to ensure they were free to make whatever choices they desired and, even if it seemed to me that they were making a mistake, I was categorically forbidden from commanding them to alter their decisions. It was entirely up to them which direction they would follow on this, their shared journey down their chosen life path.

During the height of their deliberations, I was allowed to show them the pros and cons of everything they were thinking about and to provide insights and instances for each of those cases, so they could clearly consider how their actions might help to alleviate some of the sorrow and sadness that exists in the world. And then, because it isn't enough to simply recognize and acknowledge the pain of others, I was permitted to help them feel that pain as if it was their own. Such a powerful teaching tool and actually a crucial step in the maturity of any person!

I have seen it happen, time and time again, that once humans are able to "walk in other people's footsteps" they then truly understand the emotions of others. No judgements. Just supportive comprehension and true acceptance as to how and why other people are living the way they are living.

By repeatedly washing their spirits in all the different types of empathy, Sally and Mateo not only became aware of the perspectives of other people, but were also able to physically feel what those other people felt. After that, they could then determine the type of assistance and support that would best support those in need. This empathetic viewpoint refined their own emotional skills and in turn has served them well, then and now. The deep, complex knowledge and appreciation for situations others go through enables them to make decisions with the other person's welfare in mind.

At the same time that all this was happening, I was instructed to open metaphorical doors and windows into their minds and hearts so the sunshine of goodness would pour into their souls. This way, they would be able to not only see all that is real but also imagine all that is possible.

Then, and only then, once they had seen and felt the lived experiences of others and envisioned all the possible paths those lives could take, could they rightfully decide which direction aligned itself to their own belief system and which way they themselves wanted to walk for the rest of their own lives, choosing freely and independently of undue influence.

Blessed be. They did in fact choose the way of goodness, kindness, and benevolence. And miraculously, it all happened on a warm, sunny day when they each, at almost the same exact moment, had an epiphany that would change their lives forever. They were sitting at the kitchen table, having just finished sharing a meal, they were spending some time chatting together over a cup of coffee. As they did on many such evenings, they began by covering such general topics as the weather and the news of the day and then gradually shifted to a more concentrated and deeper discussion. Without consulting the other, they each reached back on the counter to get a few of the books they kept stacked up and ready for just such a moment. Taking turns, first Sally would open one of the books to a random page of meditative thought, read it out loud and then the two of them would share their reactions to what they had just heard.

As Mateo reached out and placed in front of him yet another of the books, one that was filled with meditative inspirations on how the spirit of love can fill the soul and help a person to reach out and do great things in this world, a mild wind blew through the open windows in the room. Mateo opened the book but took a moment before choosing a page. The breeze coming through the room caused the pages of the book to rustle, then fall open. Sally and Mateo looked at each other in amazement.

Mateo picked up the book, laughed and said, "Well, I guess this is the page I am supposed to read." Sally also laughed and then encouraged Mateo to go ahead and read it out loud.

While he read, Sally put down her pen and stopped taking notes. Instead, she leaned forward and her jaw dropped in awe at what she was hearing. When he finished reading the passage, Mateo looked up at Sally over the book he was still holding in his hands. It was slowly dawning on them that perhaps this message was going to serve as their personal source of inspiration.

"We've read this page before, haven't we?" he asked Sally, who found it hard to speak so only nodded, instead.

"Yes, we sure have," replied Sally once she recovered her voice, "but honestly I don't remember ever feeling this way about anything we have read before!"

Mateo nodded in agreement and then the two of them began to talk about how they finally comprehended that it wasn't enough to just care about people and to try to give them what you would want if you were in that same position, instead it was essential that you put yourself in their position so that you could truly understand their lives as well as their desires and needs from their own perspectives.

Over the years, Mateo and Sally would tell this story to others about how that evening sitting at the kitchen table changed their lives. When they got to the point of explaining how they came to a place of understanding and discovery about their mission on Earth, their story would always harken back to how a thin but powerful book of meditative thoughts served as the guiding light for them both.

And each time I hear them relate this tale, I feel both a sense of peace within myself and a sense of pride for both of them. I am at peace because I know that I was able to do what I could to sow the seeds of thought into their heads and hearts, for I was the breeze coming in through the window. And I am proud because I know that for all the numerous times that humans are in the presence of those who guide from above and are shown the way, they mostly tend to ignore the signs right in front of them and instead opt to hold tightly onto their long-held beliefs. But Sally and Mateo were given the chance to think about what happens when you live in love and when you decide to support others by giving people what they need (as opposed to what you might think they need). They were thinking about one of the most important tenets of the world and instead of turning away from it, chose to dig deep enough to find and honor that ideal. Inspired and touched by such a critical notion, they felt inspired to move forward and to pursue the mission they felt was destined for them.

Now, I am not so bold as to think their change in lifestyle and professional purpose was my doing. Yes, I was permitted to open their minds to receive the message, but honestly just because I brought the breeze in through the open windows and just because I flipped the pages to land on that one particular page about the Golden Rule, it was their decision to read that page and it was their interpretation of the message of the written words that enabled them to see how critical it is to empathize instead of merely to sympathize.

All credit, honors and kudos go to Sally and Mateo. While each alone had searched for many years, truly from the time they were both young children, to find a purpose to the lives they were leading it turned out that here, on this seemingly ordinary evening, together they were able to find and agree upon that purpose.

In recounting their story, Sally and Mateo contend that they both shivered just a bit that evening while Mateo was reading the thoughtful prose out loud. Unbeknownst to each other at the time, and only revealed as they first told this story to some of their family members, they each contended that they felt the call of the Spirit of their God fill their hearts and souls. They say that when they looked at each other, it was only then that they noticed tears welling up in their eyes. And that shared look told them all they needed to know and, amazingly, what they knew was that not only would they answer the call to service that they had been feeling, but that they finally understood how to go about doing so. This one single passage, above all others in that book of meditative thought and in all the other books piled up in the stack of thoughtful readings that they shared together, showed them the way to fulfilling a life-mission focused on serving the needs of others.

"Let's create a safe haven for children!" Sally hurriedly exclaimed.

At that exact moment, Mateo began speaking very quickly, "A place to offer therapy for children!"

"Thought-Click!" they both laughingly shouted out, which was their inside joke for times just like this, when they had the very same thought at the very same time.

Then they sat in silence for a moment, holding hands while trying to imagine more about how and where they would fulfill this mission. They came to call that evening their own personal "Night of the Epiphany" because it finally brought light to their vision. Slowly, and with much thought and shared discussion, they began to envision working with a herd of horses because they both believed that carefully chosen, gifted horses have within them the power of providing healing to children in need.

And after they agreed upon the magical potential of equine therapy, imagining specifics about the type of place they needed to make this dream come true started to come easily. They knew the horses would need to live in a stable where they would be safe and comfortable. And they knew that not only would those horses need to be fed in their stalls but they would also need a place where they could be taken daily so they could graze outdoors, as well. It was quickly becoming clear that moving out of the suburbs and onto a working ranch was going to be the first logical step in fulfilling their new life-plan.

Before they could even think about offering equine therapy, they realized that they needed to ensure that owning and operating a horse ranch was within their purview. With that notion in mind, they dipped their toes into this new venture of ministry work by first renting a ranch that came with a couple of horses and was located very near where they were already living in New Mexico. They knew right away that while this place was not what they wanted, at least it was a start. Because this particular ranch was actually an old rodeo ground, it only had one big arena on the property and no open fields of any kind. They both knew that once they bought their own ranch, they would need to have wide open grass fields and dedicated manicured trails. Their horses had to get out of the small space of the corral on a regular basis. Spending time out in the open would make sure their horses wouldn't become anxious or stressed out, which would be a totally inappropriate state of mind if they were to be ready to work in a loving and compassionate manner with children! The horses they were going to choose had to be pampered just a bit more than most other horses so they would be relaxed, calm and capable of working with very young children.

For now, though, this rented ranch needed to serve its purpose, which was to help Sally and Mateo determine if establishing an equine therapy ranch of their own was realistic or the best use of their skills and abilities. To do that, they had to figure out how to make this property support this current stage of learning. They easily took to the daily routines of feeding and grooming the horses and enjoyed keeping the stable clean. To compensate for the lack of fields where the horses on this ranch could run and roam, they brought them into the arena every day. At least this way, they knew the horses could walk around freely and be given some sense of the outside world. Interestingly, they noticed that this arrangement allowed the horses to get to know each other and become somewhat close and attached, just like herds do when living in the wild.

Surely this place didn't fit their vision of all that they needed, but at least it was a beginning and they made the best of things as they began their initial foray into figuring out all that would be required of them. After a few months, they knew they were not only capable but were totally ready to find and establish the equine therapy ranch of their dreams. But, finding the perfect ranch was neither a quick nor easy task. As they began searching high and low for the ideal homestead, Sally and Mateo realized just how difficult it would be to find a ready-made ranch that suited their needs. They came to understand that this was not going to be one single step to their plan but would instead become a series of steps to reach that one goal.

Little did they realize that their journey would take them out of the United States, Sally's country of birth, and bring them to live in Mateo's home country, Mexico. It actually happened most naturally, for once they began sharing their idea of opening an equine therapeutic ranch with all their friends and family members, they began getting lots of leads about possible properties.

One of Mateo's cousins told them about a ranch for sale that sounded like it had great potential. It was near the beach in San Carlos, a beautiful city located in the Sonoran region of Mexico. Since it was only a day's travel from the southern border of New Mexico, they decided to head down to look at it in person. Mateo's cousin hit the nail on the head, for even though it was currently pretty run down, it was filled with potential. There was enough room on this ranch to build a house of their own, a few outbuildings, a huge barn, a grassy paddock for their horses, and an expanse of wide-open land beyond with plenty of trails where they could go for walks or rides.

After much thought and prayer, they purchased that ranch. But before they could start using the property as they wanted, they had to design and construct a house for themselves and renovate the other buildings to suit their needs. In the meantime, they moved a small house trailer onto the site so they could oversee construction.

One thing that Sally and Mateo realized, right from the day of purchase of the property, was that as perfect as this new place was going to become, it would be way too large for just the two of them to handle, so not long after they settled in, they began hiring helpers. I was allowed to provide access to many appropriate choices but the final decisions were left entirely to Sally and Mateo. They knew that they had to choose these workers carefully, for it was not enough that they were qualified to do their jobs, but it was essential that they also understood the purpose and supported the mission of this particular therapeutic ranch. In rapid succession, they were able to find such people. First came the foreman, who watched over the horses and the other workers, and then came some ranch hands, who helped with the construction and upkeep of all the buildings, arenas, fences, and trails. When the roster of workers was filled, Sally and Mateo felt at peace knowing that each person they hired was meant to be there.

A place for everyone and everyone in its place. Yes, indeed.

Even with all of the staff pitching in and helping, it still took a while to make the whole place habitable, but one magnificent day Sally and Mateo were finally able to move from that small mobile home to finally settle into their very own house. That night, they sat on the porch of their new home sipping cool lemonade while watching the sun set over the paddock, with the shadows of the tall Mexican palm trees casting long and glorious shadows all the way from the riding path to the very chairs where they were sitting.

Breathing a deep sigh of thankfulness, Mateo turned to Sally and said, "We need a name for our property that will honor it and befit its mission. What do you think about calling this place The Palm Tree Ranch?"

Sally smiled and gave a small chuckle as she replied, "I was just trying to figure that out and now I don't have to think about it any longer because you came up with a lovely name. Yes! The Palm Tree Ranch! Yes, indeed."

Nowadays, as their dear children have long grown up and headed out on their own, you would think that Sally and Mateo lived in the main house by themselves. But that is not the case. A few years ago, they applied to be foster parents and have since opened their home to a variety of different children who get temporarily placed under their protective custody and stay as long as each child's own particular needs demand.

The ranch hands reside in the outbuilding residences, though some live off the ranch with their own families and commute to work on a daily basis. And the herd of horses have settled into the beautifully renovated barn, basking in the glory of having an adjacent riding ring where they can walk and exercise, and nearby trails where long rides can be taken.

It is a homestead built and sustained by faith, love, and above all, hope.

This is The Palm Tree Ranch.

It is the place that, according to Sally and Mateo, the Lord continues to grow their ministry. Much has been altered regarding the physical layout of the property, but nothing has been altered regarding the mission of The Ranch, which began and remains true to their original concept of never charging anything to those who receive therapeutic services.

The Palm Tree Ranch is not a profitable venture; instead, its survival is dependent upon the continued kindness and generosity of charitable donors. Even so, The Palm Tree Ranch thrives and definitely lives up to its hype. Touted as a place where no child is turned away due to the severity of medical condition, all are accepted and welcomed. This includes those who run the gamut of diagnoses from cerebral palsy, Down syndrome, spina bifida, congenital syndromes, post meningitis, encephalopathy, autism, developmental delays, to mild or severe speech delays.

Any child from 4 months to 16 years old, whether medically fragile, physically handicapped, intellectually disabled, or suffering from the damaging effects of childhood trauma such as domestic violence, physical abuse, sexual abuse, neglect, emotional abuse, abandonment, attachment disorders, and post-traumatic stress, is eligible to spend time at The Palm Tree Ranch. Following evaluative assessments, children are provided with all needed and appropriate multidisciplinary therapies, basic education, life skills, and most especially, horse therapy during scheduled daytime appointments. On the grounds of The Ranch, Sally and Mateo also serve as directors of a mobile clinic where they provide wheelchairs, walkers, and other adaptive equipment for the children who would benefit from having those items.

The ultimate goal that Sally and Mateo strive for is to provide a nurturing environment, a place that helps support and serve as a resource for healing and helping all the children and their families. There are two main goals for the program they have developed: the first is to offer help to all the children who come to The Palm Tree Ranch in a manner that not only honors and accepts, but also embraces who they are and the second goal is to nurture all the abilities and talents these children have been given so that, as they develop and grow, they will be able to live up to their maximum potential.

But, of course, even with all the services that they offer, Sally and Mateo cannot deliver everything each child needs. In those cases, they schedule appointments for medical visits, dental care, diagnostic testing, and obtaining prescribed medications. When required, they also arrange for consultations and specialized tests.

Sally and Mateo firmly believe that love and care know no borders and so the ministry work of The Ranch doesn't begin or stop at the gates of their property line. They provide additional services for families that very well might include paying for passports, obtaining visas, and providing travel expenses when their children have to be taken to the United States for expert care not available locally.

As each child is brought to The Ranch, Mateo and Sally welcome them with open arms and tell them, "We are temporarily adopting you and your whole family. We are here to bring help, hope, and our love. Your needs are our needs. We will learn from you as much as you will learn from us. We will all take care of each other the best we can."

As it turns out, the healing offered through therapy sessions isn't just for the child in need. For those children who have parents involved in the child's upbringing, support and respite are made available to help them get some much-needed rest, find strength to go back to work at their jobs, and ultimately to provide better care for their children. Siblings are invited to participate in what goes on during therapy sessions and even encouraged to take a ride on one of the horses, if they are so inclined. The goal at The Palm Tree Ranch is to address the specific needs of everyone involved so they can be active participants, getting the support needed to lead the happiest and healthiest lives possible.

From everything I have seen, over all the many years I have been here on Earth and all the multitude of places where I have served, the bond of family really does matter to humans. But whether or not the children have supportive parents or have no parents at all, they must go through the steps of rehabilitation while at The Palm Tree Ranch. And while they gain a lot by working with the people during their therapy sessions, it is when they interact with the horses in the herd that they begin to feel, and more often than not, willingly accept the signs of tangible love provided by all those working at The Ranch, and in most cases also the love being sent to them by The One Who Guides Us All. And the parents, as they see their child making startling and rapid progress, come to believe that their prayers have been answered.

To be sure, the work at The Palm Tree Ranch is constant and unending, but it is never a burden to either Mateo or Sally. They wake up every morning energized in the spirit of this mission, labor tirelessly all day offering individualized care to those in their charge, and go to bed physically exhausted, but always with a sense of peace. Ironically though, rest for the body does not always mean rest for the mind, as they are always thinking ahead and preparing for what the next day will bring or require of them.

There is an old advertising saying that has been embraced within the rock music community that "rust never sleeps" and it seems to outsiders that the same mantra could be said about Sally and Mateo. They live each day to its fullest and get more done than most people could imagine accomplishing in an entire week. Part of this is due to the strong work ethic and amount of energy they have and part of it is due to their sense of the mission. In their case, that concept of non-stop rust build-up is balanced and offset by them consistently and directly addressing the matter.

And all this work has paid off, for Sally and Mateo have indeed found a formula for spinning straw into gold. The grounds are welcoming. The animals and people living and working at The Palm Tree Ranch are content. Positive change is happening for each child undergoing therapy.

Sally and Mateo found their purpose in life and now spend their time just getting on with their good works one day after another, never stopping and never complaining.

What I admire probably most of all is that the two of them are able to find opportunities where others might find obstacles. For instance, they are constantly thinking about how they can get The Ranch to more appropriately meet the needs of the children they serve. One idea that is just now starting to come to fruition is the building of a wheelchair-accessible playground. Dreams of creating an adaptive sports program for all who want to participate are floating about, as are the notions of adding caretaker training seminars and support groups.

The ideas keep flowing and as soon as one dream becomes a reality, they just move on to work on the next item on their dream-list.

As much as Sally and Mateo are the creators of the vision, and as much as they have been putting in long hours since the very beginning of this project, they also recognize that with all the work required to fulfill their dreams and ideas, they will never be able to do it all alone. Looking forward, they know there will be a need to expand the number of professionals, therapists, and teachers on staff. And one individual setting can't provide everything the children need, either.

A while ago, Sally and Mateo figured out that the only way to meet the multiple needs of all the children who come to them for therapy was to partner with other ministries. Developing a mutually supportive relationship with these organizations, they are able to provide homes, food, water, and transportation for families in need.

A true inspiration came to them a while ago when they were trying to find a way to not only provide as much as possible to this current group of children coming to The Palm Tree Ranch, but to help to ensure that the mission of offering cost-free therapy to families in need could continue into the future. Partnering with a local university, they created a program where undergraduate and graduate students would be offered internship opportunities. Starting with two interns during the first semester led to seven the following semester. Word quickly got around campus as stories were shared about all the positive things happening at The Ranch and this particular program has become very popular very quickly. Nowadays, there is a waiting list during registration and some students who are not officially listed on the roster opt instead to volunteer during their school holidays.

Not that the work is glamorous, though, for all those who contract to come out to The Ranch on a regular basis for a set amount of time quickly get put to work doing the multitude of chores needed to keep the place running (ranging all the way from mucking out the stalls to mending fences). They do, however, also get to assist during therapy sessions (for example, by helping to spot children while they are riding on the horses and by supporting them as they go through predetermined therapeutic exercises designed to address their specific, individual needs).

These college students are not only getting credit for their work, but more importantly they are receiving real-world, hands-on experience that will carry over once they earn their degrees and head out to begin caring for the children of the next generation.

Sally and Mateo wear many hats, all the way from being property caretakers to running what has become quite a charitable institution. Lots of resources to be tapped, that's for sure, and once they figured out that they did not have to do everything by themselves and that others wanted them to succeed for the sake of the children, they began thinking of more new ideas that would help make the work they do on The Palm Tree Ranch even more effective. First and foremost, though, the center remains on providing loving assistance and healing therapy to individual children while bolstering the caretakers and families of those very same children. Mateo and Sally lean on their own faith to give them strength to carry on and that faith is rewarded with all kinds of assistance for providing everything necessary to support their efforts.

Well, now, I've described the genesis and evolution of how The Palm Tree Ranch came to be. And yes, while all the people involved are definitely essential, equal attention must be paid to the other critical and indispensable ingredient of equine therapy, which is the horses themselves. So, instead of continuing to discuss the people who live and work on The Ranch, let me help you to learn about the types of horses that will work best in this venture.

Horses, in general, are adaptable and caring animals. They give more than they get. Faithful and true, they tend to stand ready to serve without complaint. But what I have come to understand about the concept of equine therapy is that you can't just put any old horse into this setting because not all horses have the temperament to patiently and calmly go through therapeutic sessions, since sometimes they might be expected to stand still for an hour or more at a time or if allowed to walk, they must do so slowly and smoothly as they go around the paddock, stopping and starting as directed. Horses, just like people, all have particular personality traits, skills and abilities. Sally and Mateo knew this right from the start and understood that they needed to find and train horses meant for the task of providing successful equine therapy.

Part of the gentle support The One Who Guides Us All allowed me to offer was to assist in developing the herd. I scoured the nearby area looking for horses that matched the criteria Sally and Mateo had determined was needed and then helped open their eyes to the best possible choices. More "thought-click" moments came their way when both Sally and Mateo saw the potential in the same four candidates. Once these horses were in place at The Palm Tree Ranch and began their training sessions, it was clear they were meant to be there. Indeed, their own individual personality traits and backgrounds had certainly prepared them to serve the wide variety of needs which would surely arise from the children who were about to come for equine therapy.

Not only did Sally and Mateo need to choose just the "right" horses that would come to live and work on their ranch, they then had to prepare those horses for the new life they would lead and help them to carry out the behaviors that were expected of them in their new role as equine therapy animals. Each horse had to be carefully trained and guided as they learned how to attend to directions given while also remaining calm and accepting of a wide range of behaviors that very well might be evidenced in the upcoming myriad of young, sometimes nervous, sometimes angry, sometimes seemingly unresponsive riders.

It was quite a process to choose and prepare the four horses who are now living and working at The Ranch. But, instead of me telling the stories of how they arrived at this place of healing and how they work with children in need, I will step back so you can hear each of their tales right out of the horse's mouth, so to speak. Obviously, I will serve as translator, writing down and staying true to their message as the stories are conveyed to me from each horse and I will try my best not to interject my own thoughts, for I recognize this special privilege of being the intermediary between the horses and you, my dear Gentle Readers.

As the horses currently at The Ranch are given a chance to tell their own stories, you will learn how they are all finally being respected and cared for in a manner both correct and appropriate for any farm animal. And you will surely come to see how each life history has made them the perfect candidates to participate in this equine therapy program, for it is not in spite of, but is actually because of all the hardships they have endured in their personal journeys that they were able to turn it all around and tend to the needs of others.

So, without further ado, let us meet Henry Street, Valentina, Buttermilk, and Bella, in that order.

Henry Street's Story

I do not count time here on Earth using the same method as humans, but I understand their system, so I was not surprised when I recently heard someone say that I am almost 20 years old. Trust me, that may sound young to most humans but by the way I feel now compared to when I was a young colt, I believe them that I'm elderly for a horse.

I've travelled quite a bit in the two decades I have been alive. I've been bought and sold over and over, moved from one town after another and I've even been taken to live in a few different countries along the way, so I speak from experience about the general nature of both animals and people.

My one, true and unfailing conclusion is that all of us, animals and humans alike, have a basic, instinctive need to find ways to differentiate between and among each other.

As animals meet, they quickly determine friend or foe and react accordingly (and sometimes they use this knowledge to maintain the overall strength of their species by weeding out one of their own if they notice weakness or vulnerability). Animals rely on detecting the physical traits of all the animals around them to survive. Humans, on the other hand, not only take note of the physical appearance of others, but for almost the past 100,000 years, since the age of hunter-gatherers, have relied upon observed physical differences as a critical method to separate themselves into disconnected tribal societies that were also based upon proximity and shared beliefs, as well.

For all of us, be we animals or humans, as long as we fall within specifically defined parameters, we are embraced and brought into the fold. As for me, I know I'm short and stocky, meaning I don't physically measure up very well when compared to other horses. Odd thing is that I have probably double the physical strength they do and I have been a hard worker my whole life, always striving to live up to the expectations of my owners.

Oh yes, I've had plenty of owners. Over the past twenty years, for each of those times when I have been bought or traded again and again, I have had a different person in charge of my life. And with each new owner, I was given a new name. The giving of a name is traditionally done after much deliberation, thought and care, usually the name we are handed at birth serves as a "gift" of sorts. That was not the case in my life, as my name changed with each new place I was sent and most of the names or nicknames my owners decided to call me were borne of anger or hate and almost always were meant to mock me.

I will not tell you any of those former names because they only stir up melancholy feelings within me. Those names are all linked to my past and nowadays I try to stay positive, focusing on what is happening in the present, preferring not to dwell on all those troubles I had to endure before arriving here at The Palm Tree Ranch. But, in order to tell you the story of how I got this name that I now proudly answer to, and just this once mind you, I must take you back to when I was a young colt. Even though I make every effort to suppress remembrances from most of the horrid events in my past, they must be shared here to give you a full picture of my life's story.

Sad events will be told, but let me begin on a happy note. Among all my memories, this one that lingers in my mind from my early time here on Earth and always fills me with happiness. Being able to hold this joy in my heart has helped sustain me during all the rough patches I've endured over the years, but more than that, this particular memory is extra precious because it is pretty much all that I have left of my one and only known relative, she who is now long gone but who has remained the everlasting love of my life. My mother. My Mama. So dear to me, then, now and forever more.

Thank goodness I have this memory. Even now, as I think back, I close my eyes and everything about that first day of life becomes clear to me as if I was living through it once again. And the best of it all begins with my Mama. The sight of her, the feel of her tongue as she cleaned me off, the smell of her as she allowed me to nurse, the sound of her as she softly whinnied in my ear to keep me calm while I got used to all the stimulus coming at me from the outside world. We bonded so quickly and permanently. From the very first moment, it was clear that I loved my Mama and she loved me. Just being near her made me feel safe and protected. If only it could have stayed that way!

Oh dear, I don't want to get ahead of myself. Instead, I shall linger on this happy memory of the day I was born for just a while longer so I can share it all with you, most especially that despite the negative comments I would soon hear from the humans around us, how my Mama told me then, and every day we were together, that I was special and perfect, just the way I was. She often said that she was honored to be my mother and she knew that I was destined for great things. I wasn't sure what that all meant, but it made me feel comforted. And now, as I head into the later stage of my life, I finally understand and more than that, I know she was right.

But back then, on that very first day of my life, there was quite a bit to absorb. I was shaky and nervous immediately after I was born. It was through filmy eyes that I struggled to notice things around me. Once my vision cleared, my gaze came upon a man who was equally fat as he was tall. He was leaning over a fence rail next to where me and my mother were corralled. He was shaking his head and looking straight down to where I was struggling to stand for the first time ever.

Even though I never heard human speech before, I was able to understand it as easily as I had understood my mother's whinnies. The rotund man exclaimed very loudly, "This one is so ugly. Thought Rosita would give us better, but this one's going to be a runt. Don't matter, though, because he is going to earn his keep, that's for sure." And then he turned to a ranch hand who was sitting on a stack of hay piled up in the corner of the barn and said, "You-There, do your job."

You-There jumped up off the hay, wiped down the back of his pants and responded very quickly, "You know it, Boss! I'll take care of Rosita. And we will get this newborn up and working mighty soon. Don't you worry none, Sir. This little guy is gonna serve you well, even if it kills him."

"See to it," growled Boss-Sir, turning to leave the barn.

You-There came over to the two of us. He first brushed down my Mama, telling her not to mind anybody else and that she should feel proud of the good job she did birthing this new colt. Then he took an old rag, dipped it in water and began cleaning my back. As he did so, he warned me, "I know you are brand new to this world and I'm sorry to tell you this but I gotta warn you to get ready for a life of work. There's a lot to be done around here and we were counting on you to help out. Already have plans for you. The cows need to be watched and that's what you're going to do. Believe me, this Boss won't put up with any laziness. You know, they say we all come into this world for a reason, and it's my job to show you the reason you were born. You can stay by Rosita for a little while, but don't get used to it. Your mama can't protect you forever. You gotta get ready to get working soon."

His words scared me, but seeing as I was just a brand new, young colt, I forgot his warning almost as soon as he uttered it. Instead, I just totally enjoyed the passing of each day, and reveled in the glory and beauty of the world around me as sunrises slowly turned into sunsets. Being with my mother was wonderful. She fed me and watched over me and loved me with all her heart. I asked about my father shortly after I was born, but my mother seemed so sad at hearing the question that I never asked again. All she said was that she never met him because breeding took place through artificial means. Well, after hearing that, I surely had many questions but never did dare to ask because I saw how upset it made my mother. I settled on not knowing any more about it and opted to be grateful for what I did have. At least me and my mother were together, and for me, that really was more than enough, anyway.

I got spoiled from having all this time with my mother. Life was so wonderful that I began to think it would always be this sweet. We were put out to pasture each morning and brought back into the stables each evening. An inseparable pair—that's how I began to think of us. To her credit, my mother did try to warn me about what was to come but those warnings went right past me, as I was so caught up in the delightfulness of just the two of us having all this time together, frolicking and relaxing each and every moment.

If I had paid any attention at all, I certainly would have known that something drastic was in the wind because Boss-Sir started coming into the stables more regularly once I was a couple of months old. Each time he visited he would look me over, grab at my legs, lift my lips to see my teeth, rub his hands along my back and pat my stomach, then ask the ranch hand, "You-There! Come on, isn't this one ready for work yet?"

And each of those times he was asked, You-There would respond with the same refrain, "Almost, Boss. Soon as he hits three months, we'll move him to the other barn and get him trained. Don't worry, Sir, I'm keeping my eye on the calendar."

And then one day, You-There had a different answer: "Oh, Boss, I can tell that this one ain't gonna get much bigger, that's for sure. But, boy, oh boy, he sure is strong and now that he is old enough, he's ready to stop nursing and start eating hay. No need to stay by his mama for that. So, yes, sir! Today is the day for this young animal to begin earning his keep."

With that, Boss-Sir said, "Well, it's about time. I need a worker, not a slacker. And I need Rosita earning her keep, too, so no more coddling for her or this colt. Let's get going and let's get them both working. You-There, you hear me? Move him out of here today."

And so, after only three cycles of the moon, it came to be that—at such a young and tender age—I was torn from my mother. Nobody told me, but I couldn't help wonder if I would ever be allowed to visit with her again. I was walked across the field and put into a much different stable. I eventually came to learn that this one held not only me but eight other horses. It took a while for me to figure that out, though, as we were all tucked away in our own stalls out of sight from each other. Upon arriving, I was led into a tiny stall and left there on my own. I felt frightened for the first time in my life when, without so much as a glance backward, You-There slammed the door behind him and walked out of the barn.

I whinnied without stopping for hours late into that first night and then did the same each night for weeks, hoping my mother could hear me from across the field. If she whinnied back, I never heard her, which tore the hole in my heart even wider. It was only much later that I heard You-There telling another ranch hand that after I had been born, they figured "that horse Rosita" wasn't worth anything because she would probably only have another runt like me if she gave birth again, so they sent her away to the rodeo and if she didn't do well there she'd be sold for meat and maybe would wind up on their dinner table one night. They both laughed at the idea even though I could tell they weren't really making a joke. My heart felt broken.

And it was at that very moment my own life took a decided downturn. It finally dawned on me that my mother and I would surely be separated forever. I knew then and there that hope of ever seeing my Mama again was gone. It struck me hard as I realized that I was going to grow up all alone in this world. My heart ached but my sadness could not change my circumstances. All I could do was to carry on and remember the blessing I had been given of having time together with my Mama after I was born. I vowed to keep that memory alive and I have kept that vow to this very day, oh so many years later.

Whenever I think of my mother, I always think of her as a powerful and proud mare who delighted in this little runt of a colt to which she gave birth. All those days and nights we spent together were perfect. I knew I was blessed to have her in my life and she often told me how much she loved me and how, even if we should be separated, we would always be tied together through our love. Once in a while, I would take note of how I looked very different than all the other horses on the ranch and she knew I was worried because I was so short in comparison, she would lean over to whisper words of encouragement in my ear, always telling me I should be proud of myself and not worried about how I compared to any other horse. She would say that everything in this world was made on purpose and though our commonalities might bring us together, it was our differences that made us all interesting and strengthened our chances of survival.

Back then, I didn't really understand what she meant, but her words made me feel better. Oh, my Mama. She gave me so much in the short time we were together and the love we shared has kept me strong and able to continue through all these many days of my life. After we were separated, I was sure that she thought of me as much as I thought of her. Sometimes I wondered if she imagined what my life was like and I always hoped that she thought only good things, for I really wanted her to be happy. So, as much as I missed my Mama, part of me is glad that she was not around to see how hard I had to work and how much I had to endure over the years to come.

I was never given any days off nor was I coddled in any fashion. I had to learn quickly what was expected of me and if it took me too long to grasp what You-There or the other ranch hands wanted me to do, I was beaten or whipped mercilessly. One morning, and every day after that, a metal bit was shoved into my mouth, placed over my tongue and latched around my head. Sometimes that bit was too tight and ironically made me look like I was smiling, though I wasn't because nothing about that pain would make me smile. Other times that bit was too loose, which meant it slid back and forth in my mouth. Either way, the whole thing was hard to endure but You-There told me, "You gotta learn to use this bit. Otherwise, you and I won't be able to communicate."

I think You-There and I had a different notion of what it means to communicate. Now, I'm not saying that using a bit on a horse is always a bad thing. In my time of living at so many different ranches, I have seen trainers who understood how to use the bit and those horses did indeed learn how to respond to the movements of the reins. But clearly You-There was not such a trainer, for over the couple of years that I lived at Boss-Sir's ranch, all efforts to get me to understand the commands of whoever was riding on me were for naught.

Try as hard as I could, I never did understand the signals my riders were giving me when they used the reins and the bit. All I ever felt was pain in my mouth. Never could eat right when riding out on the range, either, as the bit always interfered with my tongue movements which meant chewing became downright difficult. Wads of grass often got mucked up and stuck on the bit and sometimes much later those big wads would dislodge on their own and catch me by surprise as I swallowed. I guess I was lucky I never choked on them, but having that bit improperly placed in my mouth all day, every day sure did make life sorely unpleasant for me.

I never knew what specific job I would be doing each day but I realized quickly that I was just expected to go where ever I was led and do whatever I was told, without complaint. So, one morning, without any warning, when I was loaded on a horse trailer, I just boarded without thinking about it. Imagine my surprise when the truck took off and the trip took a couple of hours. That had never happened before. Once we arrived, I took a deep breath and tried to stay calm as they led me off the trailer. Turns out that I had been driven to a new ranch.

New owner, new name, many of the same kinds of jobs I had done at my first ranch. I stayed there for a while until I was bought by someone else. And, over the years, I was traded again and again, from one owner to the next. Each subsequent change of locations seemed worse than the one before. It was clear to me that all of those owners looked down on me, which I knew for sure once they would remind me that I was "just" an animal. My worth was closely tied to what I could offer. Though I did serve as a plow horse one time, I was mainly force-ridden by most of my previous owners so I could help keep their herds of cows in check.

Not surprisingly, none of those owners ever took time to groom me properly. And certainly, none of them ever came up to lovingly stroke my mane, neck, shoulders or chest nor to feed me treats. In their eyes, I was a commodity to be used, bought and sold.

So many years of constant sorrow without a bright spot—that is until my most recent, and hopefully final, purchase. Since being bought this last time, my whole life has turned completely around, and the happiness I feel now makes it easier to let go of all the pain and suffering I have endured.

Now, finally, I arrive at the part of my story where everything changes once again. And by that, I mean everything changes for the better.

As I said, these days I make it a practice to only hold onto that one memory of time with my Mama and make sure otherwise to focus on the present day. I love where I am and who I am with now. And along with all those traumatic experiences, at each terrible place along the way they would call me by a new and often derogatory name and I've also chosen to leave behind that multitude of names. Let my painful past remain in the past. Let me move forward to a much better time. Which means, happily, we come to my arrival at my most wonderful new home and the story of how I got the name to which I now proudly answer. Yes, I now respond with joy to the current name that was given to me.

Let me begin at the beginning and share with you how I arrived at The Palm Tree Ranch. At first, all I knew was that I was being sold once again. No idea where I was going or what to expect once I got there. Something reminded me of hearing, so long ago, You-There laughing about serving my Mama up for dinner and I was half expecting that perhaps that same fate was awaiting me at the end of this ride I was taking. Nonetheless, I stood up proudly that whole time in the horse trailer and showed no evidence of worry or fear. Finally, the truck came to a halt and they opened the door for me.

I laugh about it now, but I can only imagine what those watching me must have thought as I first arrived at The Palm Tree Ranch, because I must have looked a sight. My coat was matted and dirty. As I was pulled to take the steps down that ramp. I neither looked up nor listened for danger of any kind. I had been well trained to expect the worst and knew that, no matter how cruel the punishment, the only way to survive was to accept what was dealt out. And so, figuring that I was again facing an angry and demanding new owner, I held my head bent low and did my best to avoid eye contact, lest the new master think I was being too aggressive or threatening.

Once I got off that ramp and my hooves landed on the ground, I stood perfectly still, waiting for instructions to be shouted at me or worse, to feel the whip on my back directing me to move forward. None of that happened this time. Instead, a petite slim woman walked up to me and stood on my left side, gently rubbing my mane while communicating to me through touch, through words and through soothing sounds.

Within just a few moments time, this amazing woman had figured out how to reach my hardened heart. And just as quickly, I felt some of the protective armor I had built up over the years melt away and I began to relax just a little. I didn't know it, but I was ready to latch onto someone. Deep inside of me there was a longing and need to bond with another, just like I had bonded with my own dear mother so many years ago. So, when this kind and calm woman turned away from me and began to walk forward, I walked in step with her. My movements were what you would might call more shuffling than prancing, however she didn't seem to mind. She stopped talking to me for a bit as we moved forward together and the unspoken but palpable acceptance that she offered made me even more ready and willing to follow her lead.

I learned much later that the tall handsome man who leaned over the railing watching us was married to this wonderful, sweet woman. On that first day, he kept his distance from us both and instead offered his insights from afar, saying, "Well, Sally, this one is no beauty. Just hope he takes to this new kind of work we have planned for him. What do you think, dear?"

Sally-Dear smiled at the man and replied, "Oh, Mateo, I think he will be just perfect. What do you think? Do you feel the same as I do, honey?"

Mateo-Honey smiled, too, and as he turned to go said, "Ah, doesn't really matter what I think Sally. You know best, dear, as always." The two of them laughed at that joke and then Mateo-Honey continued, "I'm leaving you to it. Hope you have fun getting to know each other."

And from that time on, it mostly was just the two of us. Me and Sally-Dear.

To say the least, my life from that point on has only gotten better and better!

That's my version of the first encounter between me and Sally-Dear. I have heard her relate the story of our initial meeting many, many times over the past four years that I have lived here at The Palm Tree Ranch and there is nothing I can add. As she tells it: "When I met this beautiful horse, it was love at first sight. He came off the horse trailer with his head hung low but when I walked over to him, he lifted his majestic head and looked directly at me with those big brown eyes, bowing his head as if to ask where have you been all my life."

And Sally-Dear was so right! I loved her from that very first moment and have grown to love her more each and every moment since. The affection we felt for each other developed almost instantaneously and, looking back now, I can see that the strength of our adoration has grown stronger and more solid over the years.

On that first day together, instead of heading directly to the stables, we headed over to the fence-enclosed field so we could take our time truly getting to know each other. We had walked around and around the ring together and then just stood near each other for a long time. It was at that point that I knew this place was different than any I place where I had ever lived because Sally-Dear reached for a curry comb that was resting on one of the fence posts. Even though the going was rough due to the horrible matting of my coat, she carefully and methodically groomed me in long, slow, loving strokes, all the while talking gently to me. The lilt in her voice was oh so calming and oh so soothing and it made me feel—for the first time since I was a young baby colt—totally relaxed and at peace.

While she groomed me, Sally-Dear explained that I was the first to arrive, though she said that there were two other horses already in the stable because they had been living here when she and her husband bought the place. She told me that there would be one more horse arriving shortly and that the four of us would make up the herd and that The Palm Tree Ranch was going to be our "forever" home. Yes, there would be work to do, but she knew I would come to love their plan and this place. She smiled as she said that it would soon become evident to me how I could use the gifts I had been given at birth. I wasn't sure what that meant because I didn't remember getting any presents on the day I came into the world, but then she went on to explain that gifts meant the things inside of me that make me special. She told me that my beauty shined through my eyes and that it was clear that, even though I had been through quite a lot during my time on Earth, I consistently persevered and always showed self-reliance, both of which were positive and strong traits that would serve me well here at The Ranch.

Those words took me back to my Mama and how she used to say almost the same thing to me. I thought right then and there that if it were possible for my own dear mother to come back to me in human form, it would have been in this very person. I quickly began to think of Sally-Dear as my mother figure instead of my owner. For me, it felt like I was going to be living with family. I felt from that very first moment when we held eye contact that, living and working together, the two of us could become a strong and indestructible team. And the relationship we built back then has only become deeper and more meaningful with the passing of time.

Sally-Dear went on to explain that all of us, humans and horses, living on this property together really only had one main mission, which was to reach out and help others. She didn't say any more about that, instead telling me that there would be time for me to understand everything. For now, though, she added with a great big smile, it was enough just to spend time together, her and me, getting to know one another.

And while she continued to brush my coat, she reminded me that this was a chance of a lifetime for me, that it was important to let go of the pains and suffering I endured in my past and to look forward and start anew. Even though I was old in years, she wanted me to think of myself as being born all over again, and that this was the opportunity to finally figure out what my true purpose in life was and to see that what I was meant to do was all here, awaiting me. With that in mind, Sally-Dear went on to say, it was important that I start over in all ways, so she decided to give me a new name, one that would honor the work I was about to do, that would be tied to her own past and would carry with it a sense of nobility.

As Sally-Dear went on talking, telling me the story of my new name's genesis and how she came to choose it for me, I understood what she meant about those connections she had mentioned and I began to feel a sense of strength and resolve welling up inside of me. As she related her story to me, it somehow became my story and I could see, with a sense of honor and pride that the name she chose for me was not only grand, but that it felt perfect for me as I began upon the new path that I was forging here at The Palm Tree Ranch.

"My father's father—my grandfather—whose name was Joseph, came to this country when he was a child. Way back then my grandfather was only 16 years old."

I was struck by the coincidence and couldn't help myself. I whinnied in surprise.

Sally-Dear laughed and said, "Yes, I know, same age as you! Young for a human, but old for a horse. Anyway, one day his father came into the house and told Joseph to pack a suitcase with all the clothes he could fit but not to pack it so full that it was bursting at the seams. He said that Joseph should leave a bit of room in that suitcase to add in anything he thought was so precious he wouldn't want to leave it behind if he never came back to the house again. Joseph was confused but obeyed his father's orders, packing as fast as he could.

"When he was ready, and before he took his suitcase outside, Joseph went over to say good-bye to his mother. He stood behind her as she washed the dishes in the sink and gently touched her shoulder. She stiffened her back just a bit, dried her hands on her apron and lifted it to wipe her eyes. As she turned to face him, Joseph saw that she had been crying. He reached out to hug her and told her that he loved her. She was too filled with emotions to utter a word. Instead, she took his face in her hands and kissed his cheek. One of her tears fell onto his shirt and when he touched it, he felt the mark of her love in that small wet spot on his clothing.

"Joseph's father came into the kitchen and told him it was time to get going. Still no explanation and still the young boy did not dare to ask. The moment seemed so serious and important. Joseph knew that he would soon understand what was happening, but for now, it was enough to do as his parents directed. The two of them, father and son, climbed up onto their mule-drawn cart, quietly making the trip down the hills from their farm. Joseph knew that something big was in the works, but he wasn't sure what exactly was happening. Perhaps he was going to be sent to stay with his aunt and uncle who lived in a nearby town. Perhaps he was going to work at one of the shops down in the village to earn money for his parents so they could keep their farm and not worry about their bills. A great many ideas came into his head, but he never expected what was to happen next. Instead of turning onto the road leading to his aunt and uncle's home and instead of turning down the alleyway to the shops in town, Joseph's father took the grassy path and steered the mule toward the town docks.

"As they arrived at the waterfront, Joseph's father pulled the cart to a stop, turned to his young son and told him to get on the ship moored in front of them. Joseph started to ask a question but knew better than to interrupt his father, who went on to say the boy would be going to America, where his older brother, who had gone to the new country almost twelve years ago when Joseph was just a small child, would be waiting to greet him. My grandfather was taken aback and was about to say that he didn't want to go, but he had been raised to obey the wishes of his parents and so instead of arguing, he accepted his fate. He found himself hoping that this decision was for the best and comforted himself by thinking that if things didn't work out, he could always come back to live with his parents again.

"So, with a deep sigh of resignation, Joseph reached over and hugged his father, hopped off the cart, got his suitcase out of the back of the cart, gently patted the mule and walked up the gangway onto the ship, never looking back the whole time. Joseph cried as the ship set sail. He knew his father had his best interests at heart, and the letters they got from his brother describe how well he was doing in America. But Joseph still felt sad and scared. Those fearful feelings stayed with him all during that long trip across the Atlantic Ocean. When he finally arrived in what would become his new country, sure enough his brother, Roberto, was waiting there at the dock to greet him. The two of them hugged each other and then Roberto picked up Joseph's suitcase and brought him to his own home, where Joseph stayed until he found work.

"Promise and opportunity met Joseph in his new land. He was hired as a bricklayer and sent home half of his weekly wages to his parents, but even so he was still able to save enough money that soon he moved into a small apartment on his own. He worked hard, going to the construction site early each morning and coming home exhausted late each evening. Then, on a summer holiday when all the workers had the day off, Joseph went over to a lunchtime party at Roberto's house. And there, standing before him was the sister of one of his brother's friends. The most beautiful woman Joseph had ever seen, she immediately became the love of his life. She truly stole his heart and after a period of courtship, the two of them got married and together they had four children, who themselves each went on to get married and have children. I am one of the children of one of my grandfather's sons. That's how I came to be here on this Earth."

I stood very still as she told her story, trying to remember each detail. She continued to brush my coat and she continued telling me the story of my name, which I had yet to hear but already embraced, for I knew that when I heard the name, I was sure to love it since it was a name that came from her own family and was a part of her life.

"You, my sweet horse, have come to me and this ranch in much the same way as my grandfather came to this country. You were taken away from your mother at an early age and sent to live and work somewhere not of your choosing. I know you've had a hard life. But your story reminds me so much of my grandfather's story and I think the two of you are actually alike in other ways because I can see that, like him, you probably won't complain and I'm sure you will always work hard to do your best. So, with that in mind, I bestow upon you the honor of being named after the road where my grandparents built their one and only own home in America, where they lived together from when they were young until they became very old. Your full name will be Henry Street, but we will call you Henry."

My intuition about loving my new name was correct. I could see that it was not just a name chosen out of the air, and it certainly wasn't a name meant to mock me, but instead it was a name meant to honor me and my arrival here at The Palm Tree Ranch. And so, on that very day, I happily embraced my new name and now declare myself to one and all that I have been officially christened as Henry Street. But you can call me Henry.

Oh, how I wished on that very first day of our meeting each other that I had the ability to speak in the same way as humans do so I could tell Sally-Dear how much I already treasured being with her. While I can understand both English and Spanish when they are spoken to or around me, I am obviously unable to speak or sign any language developed by humans and have certainly never uttered a single discernable word or phrase on my own. Instead, because I am a horse, I rely upon a "non-verbal" form of communication to get my messages across to people. I use body movements as well as different snorts and whinnies to convey what I am thinking.

Ah, what joy and comfort it was for me to learn that Sally-Dear has been blessed with the gift of effectively communicating with horses, as she naturally accompanied her spoken word with a variety of non-verbal body movements, grunts, clicks, and soothing sounds. I had sometimes heard other horses speak of this special way of connecting with humans but always figured that they were probably exaggerating because I could not imagine ever having such a deep and easy exchange of thoughts and ideas between myself and any human. Well, that was before I met Sally-Dear. And not only was it possible, but amazingly, this connection was happening to me, right now and right here with Sally-Dear!

As I'd never experienced anything like it before in my whole life, I knew that what we had together was extraordinary. It didn't matter that me, a horse, and Sally-Dear, a human, used two completely different methods for expressing ourselves. We shared thoughts and ideas on a whole different plane. Of course, I wasn't able to speak to Sally-Dear in the spoken languages to which she was accustomed but when I made my sounds and body movements, she understood and when talked to me, I understood. Now I knew that those other horses weren't making up stories or embellishing the truth. Such connections between horse and humans were possible!

And the realization of so many other things that were going to be possible now that I would be living at The Palm Tree Ranch were slowly dawning on me. The most important one was that, during all those many years before arriving at The Ranch, I never really saw nor believed there was much kindness in the world. That is, until I met Sally-Dear. It didn't take long before I saw that my life, for the first time since so very long ago when I was just a new-born with my own dear mother, was now showered with compassion and caring. We quickly got into a pattern that we followed over the next few months: Sally-Dear would come to the barn, greet me with a treat and a brief rubdown, guide me out to the enclosed pasture where we would work together for a few hours, then lead me back to the barn for a leisurely time of grooming and before leaving, would offer me one more treat.

Thankfully, I am receiving only the very best of care now, but sadly, the ill treatment I suffered throughout my life has wreaked havoc on me. By the end of each day my muscles ache and, every once in a while, my head even feels too heavy for my body. Sally-Dear always looks out for me and has made it a habit to stop by and visit me in my stall each evening for a quick brushing and some kind words, which helps me to relax and fall peacefully asleep. As I wake up the next morning, the aches and pains usually subside for a few hours and all that sweet attention Sally-Dear gives helps me to feel ready to face another day.

But it's not just body aches from which I suffer. Damage to my teeth by the misuse of the bit now causes difficulties with my intestinal track. The bit, thankfully, has not been put back in my mouth and I've been promised that it never will be again. Most days, I happily eat the grass that is growing outside on the ground and the hay that is placed in the trough with relative ease, but there are still times when I have trouble with my digestive system and my body seems to react like it did when I suffered through all the ill treatment I had before coming here to The Ranch. On those days, I suffer from colic attacks, and though they are few and far between, they are horrific, for when I get hit with a bout of colic, there is nothing I can do but just give into the all-consuming pain. During those times of intense discomfort and aching, Sally-Dear stays by my side. She never becomes angry or impatient, but instead she seems to suffer right along with me. I can't count the hours and hours she has spent rubbing my stomach and taking me for walks to try to help ease my pain. Sometimes she regales me with stories, which are always about the good things we are doing at The Ranch and how the children with whom we work are better for their time spent among us horses. Sometimes she sings to me. Sometimes she coos to me or gently hums. Sometimes she doesn't make any sounds at all. But she always stays with me until the pain passes. It has become clear to me that she is here for me. And for that matter, so too are all the other people working here at The Palm Tree Ranch.

You may wonder how any blessings could possibly come from such periods of intense pain and suffering? Well, my friend, that is the miracle of love.

Sally-Dear and I have certainly bonded together during the good times but our relationship has grown even stronger during my times of physical anguish. Gradually, I have come to believe that Sally-Dear will stay by my side whenever I need her. I finally feel loved and cared for in a way I did not think would be possible after I was taken away from my mother all those years ago. Nowadays, my body may be wracked with pain but my mind and heart are filled with happiness and joy. Yes, the mission of The Palm Tree Ranch is that we offer physical therapy to medically fragile children, but for me the mission has gone far beyond that, as it is also a place where horses can heal, as well.

Valentina's Story

B ack in the old days, I never liked waking up early because it made the days that much longer. And those days were miserable. Now I wake up early every morning, but never before my current—and hopefully final—owners, Sally-Dear and Mateo-Honey. Just as my eyes begin to open and adjust to the sunshine for the first time each day, I hear the sweet melodic sound of Sally-Dear walking toward us and calling each of us in the herd. I wait for her to come to me and after I hear her singing my name: "Valentina, Valentina, Valentina," three times in a row, I whinny back in happy response. Being greeted every morning in such a loving manner sets a positive tone for the day's work ahead of us. And work it will be, but also such pleasure and satisfaction it will bring to us! One thing I learned since Sally-Dear and Mateo-Honey bought this ranch is that happiness can be found just about anywhere. For me, finding pleasure and satisfaction in the work I do makes each and every day worth living.

But, as I said, my life was not always so blessed. Growing up, I surely did see hard times and often wondered if I would survive the treatment (or rather mis-treatment) of my previous owner, Sir-Man.

Hard as those times were on me, though, maybe the most difficult thing to witness was the rapid decline of Sir-Man, some because it was too bad for him but mostly because of the rapid deterioration of care given to both me and my dear son, Buttermilk, who has been allowed to stay with me ever since his birth. We have been together almost a full decade already. And, my goodness, the changes we have seen in that time! Oh dear, please forgive me, for I am jumping all around and clearly getting ahead of myself. Let me start once again.

My time here on Earth started at this very ranch on which I still reside. I was born here thirteen years ago. I am what is known as a Bay Horse, easily told by my overall brown coat and the black coloration points on my mane, lower legs, ear edges and tail.

The first person I met shortly after I was born was my original owner, Sir-Man. He was in his mid-seventies at that time and knew all about horses because he had been around them his whole life. At this point he only owned a couple of horses and a bit of land, but that was more than enough to keep him and his one ranch hand busy, though.

Sadly, my mother died shortly after I was born. Even though I was pretty new to this world, I could tell something was wrong with my mama way before Sir-Man figured it out. You see, we were placed in the same stall together but she was having trouble feeding me. In fact, she was hardly eating anything at all herself. On top of that, she seemed overly fidgety, frequently looking one way then the other, kicking at her flank and belly, and sometimes even falling down so she could roll around on the ground.

I tried to ask her what was wrong but she only looked at me with eyes of love and said nothing. I figure now that maybe she didn't have a way to say goodbye because she must have felt like she was dying.

The ranch hand spoke to Sir-Man as he came into the barn a few days after my mama had started acting up. He spoke plain and simple. "Sir, this horse is in a bad way. I don't know what's wrong, but man, she really is in trouble."

"What are you even talking about?" Sir-Man abruptly asked. Even I could detect the note of anger in his voice and cowered back a bit so as not to get in his way.

"She won't eat or drink anything. Her manure is all covered with slime. I just found her laying down and had to force her to stand up."

Sir-Man went over to my mother and first felt her belly then rubbed his hands down her flank area. "Looks like she got colic. It's to be expected with a horse this old."

"You want me to fetch the vet?" asked the ranch hand.

"Nah—I can't afford his bill. Just put her in the trailer and drive her around for a while. See if that jogs her guts and fixes her. Otherwise ..." and Sir-Man stopped talking, leaving that thought hanging in the air. Instead, he shrugged, turned and walked away.

As he left the barn, the ranch hand gazed at my mother and quietly said, "That man has no heart. You're a great horse and you been a great worker for us for quite a few years." He glanced over at me then turned back and continued talking to my mother, "On top of all that, you brought this beautiful mare into the world. Now you gotta trust me. I'll take care of you the best way I know how and as much as that man lets me. Don't you worry none. What will be will be."

The ranch hand guided my mother into the trailer. As she prepared to walk up the ramp, my dear sweet mama turned and looked over her withers at me. She gave a soft whinny which I took to mean that she was saying good-bye. For now, or for always? I wasn't sure but I whinnied back to her to let her know that I loved her.

That was the last time I ever saw my mother.

The ranch hand stood in the barn as he reported to his boss the next day, telling him, "Well, sir, we didn't even get down the end of the road here before she just cried out in pain and fell down. Died on the spot, she did. Man, I really was surprised to see it happen so fast, but there was nothing more to be done, so I turned that truck around and drove to the burial pit. Dragged her out and covered her over with leaves and twigs. I'll get the backhoe and dig the hole today."

Sir-Man just grunted at the news. Then he looked at me and said to the ranch hand, "Lucky we got this one alive and kicking before that one died."

"What should we call this newborn, Sir?"

"Look here, you know I don't care what you name her. Long as she learns the way of our ranch and works hard. Name her whatever you like."

"Well, then," the ranch hand said quietly to me after Sir-Man left, "the man said I can name you. Let's see ... Your mama just died ... My own mama has been gone for many years now. So, I will give you my dear mother's name. I will call you Valentina."

I became an orphan and received my name, all before the sun set on the day.

They kept me in the same stall I was born in and my mama's scent lingered for quite a while after she was gone. It helped ease my sadness at losing her, but things started moving so quickly that I hardly had enough time to mourn her loss. Even though I was just a young colt, Sir-Man declared I was old enough to "get out there and earn my keep" and so I was harnessed to a wagon and led into the nearby field.

Beside me, there was only one other horse now living on the ranch. He was old and no longer strong. He had certainly done his share of work during his time on that ranch but wasn't able to take on heavier tasks anymore. He knew what I was in for and explained to me all that they would expect me to do out there in the fields, but even though he tried to warn me, I didn't truly understand what the job would entail until I began living the day-to-day life of a workhorse.

Fortunately, it turned out I was strong enough to pull the wagon, even when it was fully loaded, but one thing I had trouble with at first was the standing still and waiting patiently, which was necessary while whatever crop was ready for harvesting was gathered. That was tough enough but then I needed to be careful not to become skittish as things were flung into the wagon that I pulled behind me. Over the next few weeks, I learned how to "hurry up and wait" and so within a short time the routine of each day became familiar. Turns out, even though I never would have known it before I started working, I was actually well suited to this kind of task. I have a naturally calm and docile personality so there was no trouble in that regard and I did what was asked without ever outwardly complaining.

The ranch hand often told me what a great asset I was to him. I wasn't sure what that meant, but it must have been something good because he seemed happy that I was there to help him out and he always took lots of time to rub me down and make sure I got plenty of food and water each evening when we got back to the barn.

Now, it's true that going out there every day into the fields was really demanding work and I never did get any days off to just lie about or graze in the fields, but I soon got used to the routine and, in a way, even came to embrace my lot in life. I loved being out in the fresh air and especially enjoyed our lunch time breaks, when the ranch hand would always first rub my mane and then feed me a treat of an apple or carrot. Then he would pull out his guitar from the wagon, sit under the shade of a big old Mexican Fan palm tree and play music. We both relaxed and enjoyed our break, even though it was always shorter than I wished. Then, back to work.

I know now that I was able to carry those heavy daily loads mainly because I was young and strong. And anyway, it was all for a good cause, as I came to learn those crops being grown and harvested fed the people living on the ranch and the brush and fallen trees collected were used to light fires in their homes. I figured each daily harvest was light compared to what it could have been. At least that's what I told myself on those days when the wagon got loaded higher and higher, right up to the very top before we would head back towards the barn.

Wake up, get harnessed, pull the wagon out to the field, wait while it got loaded, haul that wagon back to the barn where I was unharnessed, groomed, fed, then left alone to fall asleep. Next day, do it again. Once you are in a routine, it's hard to notice the passing of time. I knew I was getting older but had no way to track how many days were coming and going. Same thing every morning, every afternoon and every evening until one night Sir-Man came into the barn and pointed directly at me. He announced loudly, "Time for this one to come in from the fields."

Could it be that just like that, my job pulling the wagon was ending? I thought maybe I heard wrong or that Sir-Man was joking, so I looked over to where the ranch hand was standing and to my surprise he was nodding in agreement. That made me feel even more upset because I didn't understand what was happening and I was worried that maybe I had done something wrong to make them decide I couldn't go out into the fields anymore.

The ranch hand actually cleared it up, though, when he replied to Sir-Man by saying, "Yes Sir, you know it, man. Time for this mare to become a mama."

Very soon, a stallion was brought by horse trailer over to the ranch. I hate that neither Sir-Man nor the ranch hand ever once said that horse's name out loud; I did hear them call him a "stud" but I knew that wasn't his real name. I welcomed his arrival and thought it would be good to have yet another horse around the ranch, but I soon realized he was not meant to stay. Instead, it became clear that he was brought here with one purpose: to breed with me. That stallion never did care about getting to know me at all. He just arrived one day and was gone the next. He never tried to communicate with me and certainly no love or affection was exchanged between us. It's not a part of my life I dwell upon, but I do hold the sweet memories of carrying a foal inside of me and then birthing him almost a year after that stallion's visit. And beyond that, getting to stay near my dear baby as he grew up. Yes, these are the blessings on which I focus.

Buttermilk. The joy of my life. My one and only baby. I learned later that Sir-Man had intended to sell Buttermilk as soon as he was weaned, but because the other horse living on the ranch died, I would have been all alone if he sent Buttermilk away. Horses are very social animals and need to be around other horses, never left separated and isolated, so it was with great reluctance that Sir-Man decided to let

Buttermilk stay with me. What a blessing that was for my life! No matter what the future held for us, good or bad, I knew we could make the most of it because we had each other. For that, I am grateful to Sir-Man forever more. It's too hard for me to talk about the bad times that came toward the end with Sir-Man, but Buttermilk doesn't have such difficulties, so I will let him tell his story and all the woes we went through before coming to this time of peace and happiness now that Sally-Dear and Mateo-Honey own this place, which is now called The Palm Tree Ranch.

Buttermilk's Story

My mama already told all about how she came to be in this world, and since I'm her baby that means you've already heard a little bit about me. Let me tell you the rest.

I was born on the very ranch that was first owned by Sir-Man and then later bought by Sally-Dear and Mateo-Honey. Though I am ten years old now, I was definitely way younger than that when those two wonderful humans began looking for a location where they could establish a ranch of their own. They came to see this spread where me and my mama lived because it was for sale. What's odd is that by the time they got here everything all around us was broken-down and falling apart, but something about what they saw appealed to them. I thank my lucky stars they decided it was the right place for them.

This ranch wasn't always in such terrible condition, though. Back when I was born, this ranch was in a much better state because Sir-Man, who owned the spread, kept it up, but as I grew up and became a young colt, it became evident he was starting to feel his age. It was about then that his son came to live here and together with their one and only, ever-faithful ranch hand, those three managed to keep up with all the most critical caretaking chores.

They shared the workload, taking turns to go all around the property, always checking and making minor repairs to the fences and the barn before anything would turn into a big problem. They continued to plant and weed the vegetable garden that was located out in the fields and collected the hay when it was ready to be gathered.

Someone always stopped by each morning to make sure there was plenty for us to eat and to fill the trough with fresh, clean water.

As I got a bit older, I also got a bit stronger, and that fact clearly didn't go unnoticed. One day Sir-Man announced that I needed to "earn my keep" which made my mother's ears perk up since she had heard those same words before being sent out to the fields pulling a wagon every day many years before I was born. We thought that same fate awaited me, but boy oh boy, were we ever wrong! Sir-Man told his son that my mother could get back out into the fields but that I was going to be on the rodeo circuit. No way to fight that decision but I worried because I knew that even though my leaving would bring money to Sir-Man and that was good for the ranch, it also meant that my mama would be all alone, without any other horses there on the ranch. And that wouldn't be good for my mama. Thankfully, at the very moment I was thinking those thoughts, Sir-Man's son told his father that because I would be out on the road for long periods of time, another horse should be brought to live here. Sir-Man agreed and shortly before I left, I got to see the horse trailer pull up and not one, but two horses got unloaded and brought into the barn. It was another mama and baby pair; this mare came with her own young foal.

The number of horses there at the ranch doubled in size, all in one day!

At first, I was relieved to know my mama wouldn't be alone while I was away, but within a short time it became clear that those two horses were pretty much going to keep to themselves. And, because they were both used as work horses, they would have little time or energy to socialize with my mama even if they wanted. I became more and more upset because I knew the arrival of these two horses wouldn't help my mama get over feeling lonely from missing me while I was gone.

Thankfully, my mother saw the situation a whole different way and told me she actually liked the idea of having other horses in the barn, even if we all were never going to become close allies. She reassured me and told me not to worry about anything, that I should just go out there and be the best rodeo horse in the whole show.

Over the next few days I heard, over and over, how my mama felt relieved just to know some other horses were around and then she would kind of joke that she knew they would never be friends and that she thought of them as "warm bodies" because they never were going to be very sociable with me or her. She didn't blame them, though, and told me they acted that way mainly because they had each other, exactly as we had each other. Now and forever. Even if we were apart from each other, we would still feel our love for each other no matter the distance.

I accepted my mama's viewpoint about these two new horses and once I saw how things were going even became grateful that they were there, mainly because my mama never did have to go back out into the fields. The new mama and her young colt took over that chore. Turns out my mama's only job from that time forward was to be ridden by any one of the three humans living here when one of them would go check the perimeter of the property or even rarer when one of them would decide to head out on a warm summer's evening to watch the sunset as it filtered through the palm trees located at the edge of the ranch.

My mama liked to remind me that she used to be a work horse and when she talked about what was expected of her back in those days, she always focused on how exhausted that work made her and how every evening it was all she could do to just eat some food and drink some water before she would fall asleep for the night. Then she would talk about those two newcomers to our ranch and would say that even if they wanted to hang out and chat with her, working in the fields meant that they wouldn't have much energy once they were brought back to the barn every night. I chose to take my mama at her word and trusted her when she told me what she was thinking and feeling; I believe my dear mother was truly content just knowing that mama-baby pair was around. So, even though I had no choice about going, I opted to head out on the rodeo circuit willingly and did my best out there. But each season before I was loaded on the trailer and driven away, I needed my mama to once again convince me that while the two of us were separated, she would be okay.

And in the beginning, whenever I returned, no matter how long or short a time, I was beyond happy to see that the place still looked like it was being kept up well. And my dear mama, who by now was mostly staying put in the barn, would tell me that the owner, his son and the ranch hand were working hard at taking care of everything, especially the horses living on the ranch. Then my mama would catch me up on all the news of the place, which generally didn't take very long since usually not much happened or changed those times when I was away.

After I had been working the rodeo circuit for quite a while (I guess what would be called several years in human time) I started to notice that, upon my homecomings, things on the ranch were changing, and not for the better. At first, I figured maybe it was just because Sir-Man was getting on in years—he was definitely slowing down, but sadly he also didn't seem to care about us horses anymore. Mama, who understood a lot about family relationships, told me that perhaps it was because Sir-Man's son had recently moved away, and I think she was right because once he left, it seemed the spirit was sucked out of the old man. I never did get to know why his son left. Sir-Man never came to the barn to spend time taking care of us horses so he never did talk with us about anything and I never once heard the ranch hand ask him about it, at least within my earshot.

The changes around the ranch didn't seem too bad at first, but then quite unexpectedly and quite quickly things changed from bad to worse. Those two other horses living at the ranch were sold off and we heard they were sent to two different places. Mama and I felt sad for them at getting separated but we were glad they had been able to live together for so long. Then it hit us. We realized that maybe we were destined for that same fate. Oh yes, we worried, but worry didn't help at all because we were powerless to do anything about the situation.

All we could do was fret and wait. So, we did both. Guess it worked because, amazingly, nobody came to get either or both of us. We just stayed there on that ranch, day after day, worrying and wondering.

As rodeo season approached, me and mama tried to prepare for getting separated once again. Another surprise twist, for it turned out that my rodeo days were over. Not that I was ever told so directly, but I heard the ranch hand share the news with my mama all about it one day while he was grooming her. He said, "Well, Valentina, I bet you are one happy mama now that your baby Buttermilk is done working the circuit. Enjoy your time together. Never know how long that will last because it's up to the man and not me. So, girl, enjoy it while it lasts!"

And enjoy it we did. Well, at least we enjoyed the being together, if not everything else that happened to us along the way.

How mama and I survived not being sold when all those people came to buy and take away the different pieces of farming equipment is beyond me though I sure am grateful that when it was only just two horses left in that mostly empty barn, it was me and my dear mama who were standing there. Looking back, we should have seen what would happen next but guess we were in denial about how bad our circumstances were becoming. And by the time we figured it out, conditions were almost intolerable. Even so, mama and I kept saying that it was better to deal with what we knew and definitely best to deal with it together. That's what me and my mama believed back then, and what we still believe even to this day, though the skies are way brighter now than they were then!

We knew we were hitting rock bottom on the day that Sir-Man and the ranch hand stood in the barn talking together. Sir-Man began by saying, "No beating around the bush. I think we both know it. Things are changing around here."

The ranch hand lowered his head and let out a deep sigh. He said nothing but slowly looked up into Sir-Man's eyes, held his gaze for a moment and then nodded.

Sir-Man spoke without emotion, so I couldn't tell if he was sad about it or if it just didn't bother him when he told that hard-working man who had served him so loyally for so long, "I'm going to have to let you go. Not that you aren't a good worker—don't think that, because it's not that at all. I just can't afford to keep you on. It's only me responsible for this ranch, now that my boy is gone. I gotta save all the money I can. I'm getting on in years but I don't imagine I'm dying anytime soon. Wish everything was different but it ain't. It's just the way it is."

The ranch hand stood silent all that time, still looking Sir-Man in the eye. Then he turned his gaze down for a while, shuffling one foot back and forth in the dirt, kicking up a bit of dust along the way. When he finally did look back up, I could see there were tears in his eyes. "I understand, Sir. I'm young enough and still strong enough that I know I can get other work. But I sure am sad to leave this ranch and most especially am sad to leave these two beautiful horses." And with that, he turned his gaze toward us, walked over and patted us each with more affection than I can ever remember receiving from a human in all my years of being alive.

That little show of affection and the possibility for more was what I held on to for a whole year's time because once the ranch hand departed, we were left to the care ... or actually what I call the "un-care" ... of Sir-Man. Truth is, we were basically abandoned and almost completely neglected. Because I stopped being sent out on the rodeo circuit, I was home at the ranch with my mama all the time now. What should have been a wonderful time for us was the exact opposite. We were dependent upon Sir-Man, who was the only one still living at the ranch. And any one man, even a healthy young man, would have a hard go of it trying to keep up with all the regular day-to-day work that was required, let alone also having to deal with ailments that came unbidden and unexpectedly to us horses.

It isn't like Sir-Man didn't try. At first, I blamed him for all our woes and felt like he didn't even care about us or anything any more. He made what I would call the minimal amount of effort possible, and it caused me to become angry about being constantly hungry and dirty and having to go way too long between getting chances to walk outside to feel the warmth of the sun and to breathe the fresh air. My mama was just starting to understand what it was like to be getting old and so she was kinder in her thoughts toward Sir-Man than I was back then. Whenever I complained, she would tell me, "He is doing the best he can. At least he hasn't totally forgotten us."

It was odd that somehow, even with less horses around the ranch now, there was also lots less food available for just the two of us who were left. And what food there was wasn't coming quite as consistently as it used to be. Our trough was almost never filled with fresh water. If we were lucky, once a week or so, we would watch that old ranch owner hobble over to the stalls. When he opened the gate, we were permitted to walk over to the corral. At that point, he would throw a little bit of hay down in our stalls then come outside and send us back into the barn. The first few times this happened, we gobbled it all up very quickly because we sure were hungry, but after a couple of weeks of seeing that everyday walks or more importantly, delivery of hay wasn't guaranteed, we started to ration the food given in case lots of time went between servings. As for water to drink, well that was another sad story. The old cement trough that used to be filled every day now pretty much only held water that came from the skies when it rained. The constant low levels in the trough meant that whatever water there was would rapidly turn smelly and get covered in green algae.

The stable that once was sturdy and strong had deteriorated to such a state that there were holes in the roof. We knew that good and bad things could happen at once, so even though the rain would bring us water to drink, it would fill up our living quarters, turning the dirt beneath our feet to mud that never seemed to dry up completely. That damp muck stayed around, and even built up until it eventually rose to a level just below our knees.

I know that humans count time differently than we horses do, and I surely never did learn how to use a clock or a calendar, but I could tell by the number of sunrises and sunsets, along with the changes in the moon that back when things were good, we had our shoes redone pretty often. I once heard Sir-Man brag that we got them fixed "every six weeks, like clockwork." But once Sir-Man was left alone on the ranch, what he called weeks and then what he called months would pass by without him once even looking at our hooves, let alone taking care of them.

At first, we tried to rail against such horrid treatment, but after a while we didn't even really complain any more. Slowly but surely, we kinda gave into the miserable conditions and wallowed in the muck and the sorrow we felt at being ignored. We figured this was our lot in life: to live in such miserable conditions and then die. Sometimes I wondered if it would be better if Sir-Man would just open the gates completely and let us go wild on our own. Trying to survive out there in the world couldn't be any harder than what we were going through here at Sir-Man's ranch.

And then one day, when me and my mama were feeling about as sad as sad could be, out of the blue, this woman and this man we had never seen before came toward us. We could tell by how Sir-Man walked with them, smiling and talking about what great horses we were, that something was definitely in the wind. Almost immediately, and without even looking at each other, my mama and I both perked up as they approached where we were standing.

Friend or foe? That was always the first thing we had to decide each time any new animal or human being came near us.

Fight or flight? Would it be necessary for us to stand our ground and run up against the enemy or should we be looking for a way to escape?

Ever since I switched from being a baby colt to a stallion, I took on the role of protector for my dear mama. So, there I was, standing at the ready, my ears pinned to my head and my eyes darting back and forth between the man and the woman, watching carefully as they approached. Step by step, as they got ever closer, I used all the alert-ready skills I had honed over the years. I knew that even though I was still relatively young, my time working as a rodeo horse would serve me well. What made me good at that job was that I was very fast and not afraid to be aggressive; I loved to chase down a calf in no time, watching with delight as my rider hopped off me to quickly rope it. The audience would clap and cheer at how well me and my rider did. I would hear chants of "Buttermilk! Buttermilk! Buttermilk!" rise up from the audience and then my rider would come over to stand next to me, always beaming with pride.

Didn't matter that nowadays I was locked almost 24-7 in a small stall; I still had tons of pent-up energy in me that reached all the way to the depths of my core. Being left shuttered up and unused for so long, once the adrenaline starting pumping through me at the sight of these strangers and the urge to run or fight kicked in, I quickly remembered how great it felt to let myself go and give in to those feelings. I stood ready to prove to myself and everyone else how strong and fast a horse I really was deep inside.

I knew that my size and general appearance surely added to the ability I had to intimidate others—compared to most ranch horses, I am what is considered to be a big horse. In addition, the deep overall black color of my coat has always made me somewhat scary to most people, especially to those not used to being around horses very much. Of course, I often thought that the little bit of white that was on my two back hooves offset all that scariness, but honestly nobody tended to notice that particular feature very much or if they did, they didn't interpret my unique coloration the same way as I did, or at least they never commented on it in front of me.

Yeah, I wanted everyone to think I was tough. What else did I have going for me? Well, over the years I came up with some other warning cues to put off those who would try to get near me. Not only would I pull back my ears and stare people right in the face, but I pawed at the ground and snorted in such a menacing way that I knew it even gave pause to those who might have been around horses their whole lives. Truth is that deep down inside of me I always felt excited and pleased about being able to intimidate others.

So, that morning, as these strangers approached, I used every trick in my arsenal to get the upper hand on them.

Despite all of my noisy antics, I still could hear the exchanges taking place between the woman and the man. They spoke to each other as if Sir-Man was not even there.

The woman began, in a voice choking with emotion, "Oh, Mateo, I am sure those horses are beautiful on the inside but honey, they sure do look dreadful on the outside. I can't stand imagining what they've been going through. Do you think there is hope for them? Do you think they can be saved? We have to do something for them!"

The man reached over, took her hand and replied, "Oh, Sally, I'm seeing the same thing you are, dear, but I think we can nurse them back to life and then they are going to be beautiful both inside and out. And I feel confident they will be able to help us with our mission."

Getting ever closer to the stable, Sir-Man finally started talking directly to those two people, "Now, Sally and Mateo, I know it might look kinda bad, but you gotta remember that I haven't been well and that I'm here all alone. I've done the best I could. You gotta trust me that these are two hard working and really capable horses. Valentina pulled a wagon for many years and this baby of hers, Buttermilk, went on the rodeo circuit. They got skills. Now, I'm telling you and you can believe me, I know you'll be happy moving here to the ranch and even happier with these two working for you. Buying this place is quite a deal. And I'm not just saying it because you caught me just as I decided it was time to sell, either."

Sally-Dear and Mateo-Honey looked at each other, then slowed down their pace so they could take their time getting to us. I was sure they would both feel a bit panicky and definitely afraid once they saw me and my menacing ways. Well, at least I thought that until Mateo-Honey looked directly at me and laughed out loud, saying, 'Buttermilk, you sure are trying so hard to be mean. But I can see right through you. Relax. We aren't here to hurt you or your mama. It's the opposite, boy. We're here to take care of you and to give you a chance to take care of others."

I wasn't exactly sure what Mateo-Honey meant by that, but I could feel my heart begin to beat a little slower and my breathing start to calm down, too. In all my born days, this was the first time I ever connected with any human so quickly.

I turned to tell that to my mama, but I knew right away she was feeling the power of the love emanating from this pair of humans just as much as I was. By the way those two were making eye contact, I could see that my mama was starting to bond with Sally-Dear in just the same way as I was with Mateo-Honey.

Sir-Man murmured something about his legs hurting and how hot it was outside and how he needed to sit down in front of the fan to cool off. He turned and waddled off, away from the four of us. Mama and I looked at each other. We were trying to figure out what was going on. We thought it might be good news, but we were too afraid to dream such a thing could be true. Sir-Man had gone into his house and now here we were, just two horses and two humans. Keeping our distance, we all seemed to understand getting to know and trust each other wasn't going to be an easy task because I gotta tell you, by the time Sally-Dear and Mateo-Honey found us, me and my mama were both doing poorly. We were exhausted and damaged, both physically and emotionally.

Even though the two of them tried to show no emotion as they calmly and slowly inched toward us, Sally-Dear seemed to reach a breaking point once she got up close enough to really see how we were living. She took one look at us standing there in our muck-filled stalls and her eyes teared up. She turned away for a minute, and then said to Mateo-Honey, "This is a disgrace. It's beyond that. Oh Mateo, I can barely stand it. How have these horses been allowed to live like this? You know, honey, it's no wonder they are in such distress. We will have our hands full taking care of these two, won't we?"

Mateo-Honey didn't say anything but instead reached over and gave her a hug.

Both me and my mama were a bit overcome with mixed-up emotions, too. Deep down we wondered if there was something about these two humans that was worth believing in, but we had experienced too much sorrow for too long and just turning ourselves over willingly to this couple felt almost impossible. What was happening? Had they really come here to help us?

For me and my mama, having suffered so much, we feared that more suffering was about to happen. Pent-up anger, fear, worry and dread all bubbled up in both of us at the same time and we couldn't hold our emotions in check any longer. We let out loud whinnies and started fidgeting, getting more and more intense and rambunctious with each passing moment. We did what all horses do when they want to express distress. We became as noisy as possible. We knew that we were not being friendly and welcoming to these newcomers, especially because we resisted their attempts to touch us by backing away from both Sally-Dear and Mateo-Honey every time they started to come near. It wasn't that we wouldn't have been glad to be taken care of, instead it was that we just did not trust anyone any more.

Fortunately, Sally-Dear and Mateo-Honey not only understood horse behaviors, but for some odd reason, seemed to really like both me and my mama. They quietly stood near us for a long time, then bid their goodbyes with promises to return. We watched as they walked away, hand in hand, and figured we'd never see them again. But they came back the next day and then the next and every day they came, they stayed by our sides from sunrise to sunset. And, with all that loving attention, we gradually opened our hearts to these two people and ever so slowly a truly deep-seated loving and trusting relationship between us all was being built.

Sally-Dear and Mateo-Honey took care of us in earnest by cleaning out our stalls, bringing us plenty of food and fresh water, taking care of our hooves and getting us new shoes. My favorite part was the grooming we got every day because boy oh boy, did that ever feel good!

Sir-Man stayed for a while (a couple of full moons at least) but then one day, as a total surprise to us, his son showed up out of nowhere. We thought he just came to visit his father. He never walked over to say hello to us when he got there, though, so all we could do was wait and watch to see what was happening. Sir-Man came out of the house with a suitcase in his hand but never did come over to say goodbye to us. His son opened up the passenger side door so the old man could climb in the car. The son got behind the wheel, started the engine and they made their way down the driveway until they were out of sight. We thought at first maybe they were heading on a vacation trip, but after a good while went by and they didn't return we caught on that Sir-Man had left for good. Shortly after, Sally-Dear and Mateo-Honey brought a trailer to the property and we knew they were here to stay.

This was our new reality and we were starting to like it. And pretty soon, me and mama decided we were ready to turn ourselves over completely to our new owners. Sally-Dear and Mateo-Honey must have sensed the way we were feeling because on that very day we were both saddled up and next thing we knew, we were being ridden for the first time in a long time.

And it felt great!

We quickly became accustomed to our new schedule and the pace of our lives suited us just fine. We don't really have what you would call seasons here at the ranch because we live in a place where the sun shines down upon us most days and the temperature stays pretty much the same all year, so it really is hard for me to know how much time passed by from when we went on that first saddled ride to this next part of my story. Doesn't really matter how many days, weeks or months went by though, because time was our friend now. Me and mama were finally relaxed and completely content with our lives. We could have lived like that forever. It was clear to us that along with Sally-Dear and Mateo-Honey, we made a perfect "family" of four. Imagine our surprise, then, to hear the two of them chatting while brushing our coats one morning.

It started with Mateo-Honey, who said, "Well, Sally, dear, today is such a big day for us. Finally, we will be getting Henry Street, that old stallion, here with us. The driver bringing him will be arriving any minute now. And before you know it, Bella will be loaded up in the horse trailer and delivered here, too. We've worked so hard to get this ranch back into shape. And now it's time to get our whole herd together. I am totally confident that those two horses we're adding, along with these two beauties, are going to allow us to fulfill our mission."

Sally-Dear let out a relieved sigh and replied, "I know! Oh Mateo, how blessed we are. Soon we will have a full stable of horses. Honey, can you imagine? Between you and me and these four amazing animals, we will all work toward one common but oh, so important, goal: helping children in need."

"Amen!" exclaimed Mateo-Honey. "Yes, indeed! God is good. And because all of these four horses definitely understand what it's like to have been injured and then how wonderful it is to be cared for and to heal both their bodies and their souls, they will surely embrace the children who come here for therapeutic rides."

"Feels like a match made in Heaven," said Sally-Dear.

And the two of them laughed together in joy.

Mama and I looked at each other several times during their discussion. Nothing we could do to add to the talk they were having but when we heard the news about more horses coming, even though we were surprised, amazingly we didn't feel jealous at all. We remembered the days, long, long ago when other horses lived with us on this ranch and we figured two more horses now would be welcome company. We didn't really know what therapeutic rides meant nor did we grasp what mission they were talking about. And we really didn't care to know at that point. We were just both so happy. And hearing Sally-Dear and Mateo-Honey laugh together meant they were happy too. Wanting to share in the merriment, me and my mama each let out a contented whinny, hoping our human friends would know how we felt.

We were living the good life, but we couldn't help but notice how hard Sally-Dear and Mateo-Honey were working. Every single day, they started first thing in the morning and went all day until darkness descended, only stopping for a quick meal break around noon. They kept at it and never wavered because there was so much to be done, not only to get the ranch ready but to keep up with all the needs of us horses. Mama and I sometimes talked about it and worried that maybe one day the two of them would just give up like Sir-Man did. We wished we could help them, but knew that was unrealistic. They needed another human to take on some of the workload necessary for managing the upkeep of the ranch and of us animals.

And then, early one morning, unannounced and unexplained, everything changed and thankfully, it changed once again for the better. Without warning, a new person walked into the barn. Sally-Dear seemed a bit startled herself as she sensed someone other than Mateo-Honey had come through the door. She spun around, ready to defend herself and us, but upon seeing who it was her concern turned to delight and she walked over to greet what might be the tallest, thinnest person I have ever seen. "Gabriel! Buddy! Welcome! So happy that you will be working with us. Hope you got settled into the bunkhouse okay."

Gabriel-Buddy replied, "Yes, indeed. Nice accommodations. Thanks for fixing it up for me. I'm looking forward to getting started helping out. What you need me to do, Sally?"

"Well, you, as usual, have perfect timing! Come meet our fine horses. This," she said stroking my mane, "is Buttermilk. He's a bit rambunctious but that's part of his charm. We think of him as our rebellious teenager. At first glance, watching him charge around like a wild thing, we thought he would be impossible to use for our work. Just when we thought we would give up, a miracle happened. For some reason he and Mateo bonded with each other. They locked eyes when they first met and I think at that very moment something magical happened because Buttermilk took a shine to my sweet husband. So, Mateo got volunteered by me to take over the training for Buttermilk, didn't you, honey?"

Mateo-Honey had just entered the barn. He smiled and said, "Yes, my dear Sally, yes. And believe me, I'm happy to oblige. Buttermilk and I have become great pals and he is getting calmer with each day that passes."

Gabriel-Buddy asked, "Then will I be training Valentina?"

As Sally-Dear walked over to formally introduce Gabriel-Buddy to Henry, she replied, "I think you and I will team up to train both Henry and Valentina. And because Buttermilk and Mateo bonded right from the first day they met, seems logical that those two will be working together."

Nodding, Gabriel-Buddy said, "Sounds like it's all coming together. Training these horses will be interesting, to say the least. They have a lot to learn and it will be a whole new lifestyle for them, won't it? These other two horses look like they will fall right into their new responsibilities. Only one I'm really worried about is Buttermilk, so glad you're taking over his training, Mateo. You say he's spent his whole life living with his mama? I hope he's ready to share her, not just with the other horses here in the barn but with all those children who are about to come visit us here at this ranch!"

I wasn't sure exactly what Gabriel-Buddy meant, but Mateo-Honey and Sally-Dear both nodded in agreement, and because they all knew what they were talking about, no more was said.

Instead, Sally-Dear stopped patting me and turned her attention to my mama. "And even though you've heard about her, you haven't formally met her yet. This," she said reaching over to give my mama a carrot, "is Valentina. She's worked hard her whole life. Before she had Buttermilk, she pulled the wagon here on this ranch for many years and from what I hear, they loaded it to the max on each trip to and from the fields. We've been told that she used to be energetic when she was young and even though she's slowed down some now that she's older, I know she still loves to run. Biggest blessing is that Valentina is generally calm and I'm happy to say we've already noticed how willing she is to take directions from us." Sally-Dear laughed and added, "Hopefully, some of her relaxed spirit will eventually rub off on Buttermilk."

Gabriel-Buddy looked around and asked, "I thought there were four horses in this herd?"

Mateo-Honey replied, "There will be. We're still waiting for one more horse to arrive. She should be coming in a couple of weeks. Her name is Bella. We aren't sure who will be training her yet, as we want to see how she fits into the herd and which one of us she feels most comfortable with. She lives on the ranch next door and her current owner asked if she could stay there for just a while more since her youngest colt is almost ready to be weaned."

Whoa. My head started spinning because of all of the new information being thrown at us that morning! So much to absorb all at once. Almost too much. At least too much for one day. But, as life has a habit of doing, one day turned into the next and the next and so on and pretty soon nothing was too much to absorb. What I came to see was that I didn't have to worry about anything. I was getting stronger every day with the excellent loving care I was receiving and soon I would be giving back as good as I got. And as each day passed, I started to getting a clearer picture of what these therapeutic rides might entail; I felt confident that with the guidance I was being given, I would be able to provide those kinds of rides for all the children who were about to start coming to The Palm Tree Ranch. Even though I still didn't understand everything about this equine therapy program they kept talking about, helping Sally-Dear and Mateo-Honey to fulfill their mission was quickly becoming my mission, too.

Bella's Story

I'm not the youngest—that would be Buttermilk.
I'm not the oldest—that would be Henry.

At 15 years of age, I fit somewhere in between, which means that both Valentina and I qualify as the "middle ones" of the herd.

Also, even though I was not the first horse here at The Palm Tree Ranch, I do hold the honor of being the last to arrive. Nowadays, Sally-Dear and Mateo-Honey constantly tell all four of us that there won't be any more horses coming; we are the entire lot and that means we must all learn to get along with each other.

That hasn't been an easy task, as getting any four horses to bond is a tricky thing, especially when the group is comprised of mostly "senior citizen" horses who have lived through and witnessed so much during their time on Earth! But, Sally-Dear told us we needed to get along, and we were determined to figure out some way to do it.

One thing I've learned since coming here is that horses definitely set up a pecking order amongst themselves. In my previous herd, I was the lead mare, almost by default. I didn't really want that position, but it was handed down to me when the previous mare became too old and before she could die on her own, got shipped out to be turned into meat. As most of that herd was comprised of my own children, the mantle of lead mare was handed down to me. Over time, I realized I was actually good at being a leader, so when I got brought to The Palm Tree Ranch, I just figured that I would be the lead mare here, as well.

Wrong.

By the time I arrived here, the other three horses had already determined their own pecking order and they clearly liked what they had chosen. Henry, Valentina, and Buttermilk quickly let me know who was the boss (and it wasn't going to be me, that's for sure). Henry, as the alpha-male was chosen to be the leader of this herd and Valentina, as the only female horse of the three, and Buttermilk's mother to boot, followed as second in line.

Henry took it upon himself to make sure that I understood he was the dominant force in our herd. Together with the other two horses who had been here "before my time" they figured out a bunch of ways to show me my place. I quickly learned to pay attention to all the various non-verbal signals they were offering me. I most especially tried to notice if anyone had their ears pinned back with their tails switching as I approached, for I recognized that some kind of standoff was about to take place. Anything from pushing me out of the way if I tried to get to the food first, to overtaking me and getting into the lead when we were riding the trail, to even being the first to chase a wild rabbit when we were let out to roam free on the pasture. These were all signals designed to ensure that I understood I was not in charge and never would be.

Guess I'm a bit stubborn, though, or maybe I might be a bit slow. I didn't know what was going on, so it took a long time for me to first comprehend and then to finally accept the new hierarchy, though I eventually did. And even to this day, once in a while if I dare to forget my place, the other horses remind me through their highly successful bullying and coercing tactics and I quickly get back to toeing the line.

While all these behaviors might seem harsh to outsiders, the system that horses have of deciding and keeping order in the herd is actually a good thing for us. Though adult humans might balk when they witness how we treat each other, the children who come to The Palm Tree Ranch clearly understand and buy into this notion of a pecking order. I hear them talk about us and notice that they think of Henry as the father, Valentina as the mother, me as the big sister and Buttermilk as the little brother. It's amazing to me that no matter when they arrive here at The Palm Tree Ranch, each child ends up labeling our roles in that same fashion.

And to be perfectly honest, I don't miss the role of lead mare one single bit. Less constant vigilance needed and less worrying about the general welfare of others has led to much less stress in my overall life. Although, quite frankly, I find the whole thing kind of funny about not being called the mother of the herd because back at my old ranch, I had two main jobs: (1) to get saddled up and go out with tourists wanting to ride the trails and (2) to breed. The first job was boring at best and a drudge at worst, with lots and lots of novice riders who apparently had seen one too many westerns and thought they could ride me like the cowboys in the movies, jumping up and down in the saddle, kicking my sides to make me run, and pulling hard up on the reins to get me to stop. The second job was nothing I ever thought about as it just happened and was seemingly a constant in my life, for in my hey-day I carried and birthed seven babies, one right after another.

All my babies grew up to be fine working horses and thankfully they all got to stay together at that ranch, which just so happens to be right down the road from here. I miss them, of course, but I keep in touch in my own way. On days when the wind is blowing just right, I can catch the scent of them and I close my eyes, remembering what each one looks like and it is then that I go over in my mind some special memory I shared with them, one and all.

Sally-Dear understands how much I miss my babies and whenever she takes me out for a ride on the trail, she makes sure that we run past the pasture of my old ranch. There is one favorite spot under the shaded canopy of a really tall Mexican Fan palm tree where we stop and rest for a while. It's beautiful there, cool even on the hottest of days. And it just so happens to be the best spot possible for me to have a chance to visit with my family.

As we approach that tree, we always slow down and then as soon as we are fully under cover of the tree's wide branches and broad leaves, we pause for a bit. I rear back my head and send out a somewhat wild-sounding whinny as loudly as I can, shaking my whole body to give me extra energy for that call. And my efforts always pay off, because within a few minutes, as many of my children as are available come running to greet me. I am over the moon happy to see my babies once again and they feel the same about seeing their mama! We all start nickering and that's when Sally-Dear laughs and says, "When you close your mouths and make that sound, I know you are all happy to see each other. I think I'll just sit down and rest a spell so you can spend some time together."

And with that, she jumps down off of me and goes over to lean against the trunk of the tree, sitting quietly, sipping on her water bottle, easily switching back and forth between reading whatever book she brought with her on the ride and just watching us horses enjoy being together.

And, oh! How we do love spending time catching up on all that is happening at our respective ranches! We begin by just nuzzling one another, then shift to rubbing heads against heads, chattering all the time. When we finally finish greeting and grooming one another, we just rest our heads over the necks of our dear beloved pasture mates.

Sally-Dear never hurries us because she knows how much we love our shared time. We just relax and enjoy being together once again. Eventually, she stands up and we know that's our signal that the visit is about to end. And always just before we depart, Sally-Dear goes into her saddle bag, puts away her water bottle and her book, then spends some time ferreting about inside the pouch. We all get excited when she does this, for we know that a treat is on the way. My now-grown up babies begin stomping the ground and the youngest of the brood always rears up his front legs and neighs loudly—kind of his way of showing off in front of his family.

And then the feeding ritual begins. Sometimes it's carrots, sometimes it's apples, sometimes it's sugar cubes. We never can guess what she has hiding in that bag, but we all know that it's going to be something delicious.

Without fail, Sally-Dear always holds out the first treat that will be given in the palm of her hand and walks over to me. And each time, she says the same words, which sound like a sort of prayer, "Bella, you beautiful, gentle buckskin mare—it's your earned right to go first because you are the matriarch of this herd here before us, then and now and forever."

No treat has ever tasted sweeter to me than the one I eat after she says those words!

Yes, indeed, the connection is strong to my own dear family-herd. But so is the connection I have with my new herd at The Palm Tree Ranch. My life has been blessed and living here, working with all the children who come for therapeutic rides, my blessings are multiplied a hundred-fold!

Laying the Groundwork

And now that the horses have each introduced themselves, I, Thou-Est, return to guide you, oh Gentle Reader, on the journey as humans and horses work to meld together and prepare for the mission of The Palm Tree Ranch: to provide physical therapy for children in need. This journey has been, and continues to be, dependent upon the offerings of two "regular" humans. Not superheroes, but merely a couple of people offering superb love and care for their fellow human beings. Sally and Mateo are always the first to remind anyone who asks that none of the miraculous healing experiences they have witnessed on The Ranch could have happened without that other critical piece in this triad of equine assisted physical therapy, which is the horses themselves. As Sally and Mateo are quick to say as they describe all the therapeutic recovery miracles occurring at The Ranch, "The horses are really the best therapists!"

What makes this story truly impressive to me is that although Sally and Mateo had been around horses for years in a variety of different ways, but until they established their equine therapy practice, they had never owned any horses of their own. Over the years and during many visits to the ranches of their friends, they had come to personally learn about the soothing feelings and healing power of being around such wonderful animals. They easily bonded with each horse they met and in fact, the two of them were known all around their area in New Mexico as the ones to ask if temporary caretaking of a herd was needed. Whenever someone went away on business or holiday, they usually turned to Sally and Mateo to take care of their horses in the stables.

Daily routines needed for tending to the horses came easily to Sally and Mateo, who found the required chores such as mucking out the stables, checking the water tanks, putting out hay, and exercising the horses to be both peace-filled and soul-nourishing.

Mateo would often say the thing he admired most about horses was how very observant they were. Even though he knew this was critical as a means to keep themselves safe, it constantly amazed him as to how hypervigilant about their surroundings they were. He knew that being animals of prey, not predators, horses needed to make rapid determinations based on these constant observations so they could be at the ready to react accordingly in a nanosecond. He recognized that horses had long ago honed their natural instincts to watch carefully for anything that might hurt or kill them and that being in this constant fight or flight mode increased their odds of surviving, but he was fascinated by the intense strength of their powers of observation.

Because Mateo believed that God had blessed these magnificent creatures with the ability to discern friend from foe instantaneously and with spot-on accuracy, he never failed to feel honored each and every time he was seen as a friend. Having grown up in an area of Mexico where there were many ranches, Mateo spent lots of time around horses, even as a young boy. And, more often than not, whenever he would meet any new horse for the first time, he would immediately be greeted by getting licked or being given a couple of gentle nudges. Mateo would always accept these behaviors because he understood that those gestures meant the horse was accepting his presence as a friendly being. On such occasions, Mateo would return the compliment and while rubbing the horse's back would quietly assure it that he had only the best of intentions. Being around horses was always easy and natural for Mateo.

For Sally, the thing that drew her to horses in the first place was how extremely intuitive and sensitive they were to the emotions, feelings, and intents given off by people who were around them. It was as if they knew how to behave depending on what they perceived about each person they met. And Sally knew that she was blessed, right from the very beginning, to love and be loved by horses. She often talked with great fondness about Dusty, the very first horse that she ever met way back when she was a young child. One summer, after much imploring and cajoling, her parents had finally agreed to let her to go for a week out to a riding camp in western Massachusetts. As soon as they drove up to the gates and her parents pulled up in front of the cabins, Sally and her best friend, Margaret, who was also going to stay for the week, bounded out of the car and ran over to the fenced paddock where five horses were quietly grazing in the field. One of the ranch hands came out to greet the girls, handed them each a small piece of a carrot and explained how they could offer the treat. Margaret held back, saying she was surprised how big the horses were in person and that she wasn't quite ready to get too near such a large animal yet. But Sally, who paid close attention to the directions, carefully placed the carrot toward the front of the flat of her hand, and with no hesitation at all walked over to the fence, reached her arm over the fence and waited quietly. Within a very short time, an extremely tall chestnut American Quarter horse rambled over to where she was standing, looked her in the eye, and then leaned over to take the carrot. While the horse ate that treat, Sally stood very quietly and waited. Then the ranch hand formally introduced her that the horse, who was named Dusty, and told her that if she perched herself on the small stool located outside the fence, she would be tall enough to reach over to pet the horse. Sally grinned from ear to ear and got right up on the stool. She did as the ranch hand directed, putting her hand just below Dusty's mane, finding his "withers" (which she came to learn was the fancy name for the bump at the base of his neck) and scratched, very gently at first and then a bit more assertively. Dusty leaned his head outward and then back toward Sally, letting her know he was enjoying this time together.

From that moment on, Sally was totally enamored by not only this one horse, but all horses in general.

The horses on that ranch all took to Sally and all pretty much avoided Margaret, who never did warm up to being around them. It was as if they could read the minds of these two young girls.

And over the years, Sally noticed that it was as if all horses were able to figure out a person's personality, mood, and disposition, even from a very far distance. She often saw horses react in kind when they perceived that the person was happy, loving, at peace, angry, sad, mean, aggressive, or even in pain. She couldn't really understand how horses could do this and it seemed basically unexplainable to her, but with each new experience being around horses, she noticed this mirroring happening often and each time she would come to see that the horses were indeed right on target in their assessment of the person they were meeting.

Because Sally and Mateo both had a natural liking and understanding of horses, they knew as soon as they had the idea to establish a ranch that offered therapeutic equine rides to children in need that it would be a positive and effective venture. But they also knew that it would require a lot of groundwork to prepare the horses before any children ever started coming for services. Sally and Mateo developed a plan to provide lots of attention, care and training of these glorious animals to get them ready for their upcoming mission.

Part of that training was to first help the horses overcome any distrust of humans remaining inside of them from all their years of abuse. In addition, they were encouraged to not react with the engrained negative habits they had developed over the years and instead were trained to utilize new habits that increased their patience, their tolerance of erratic child behaviors and their ability to adjust to both expected and unexpected circumstances.

Even though it might seem to an outsider that all horses are basically the same, Sally and Mateo were aware that they would react to training differently and so they were careful to get to know everything they could about each of their horses. They set about purposefully learning all they could and it was only after that gathering of knowledge was completed that they could individualize an approach to be used with each one. Sally would laugh when she talked about this approach with Mateo, always telling him, "When I was a little kid, my mom would say that all us siblings weren't being treated the same, but we were always being treated fairly. Now here I am, telling my horses that same line!"

Horses are, in comparison to relatively smaller humans, huge animals. That makes many people nervous when they are around horses for the first time. Sally and Mateo knew that many of the children coming to The Palm Tree Ranch might feel nervous or skittish, so they had to be sure that the horses stayed calm no matter how the children behaved.

From where I rested, hovering above the scene, I have to admit that I surely did enjoy just sitting back observing. And my oh my, how I came to appreciate all the different strategies Sally and Mateo employed in their training sessions! The most effective one relied upon the fact that horses are herd animals who often play the "who is most dominant" game amongst themselves. One way that horses demonstrate this dominance is by seeing which one can make the others move. Sally and Mateo figured out how to make that same concept apply to interactions between horses and humans. Now, of course the two of them didn't do this exercise in quite the same manner with the horses they were training, but the result was the same nonetheless. Despite the somewhat divergent paths they took while training their assigned charges, Sally and Mateo made sure that each horse would come to view them as equals of sorts. They knew that once it happened, the horses would willingly respond to directions they were given.

Sally and Mateo also spent lots of time feeding and grooming the horses, talking with them and making sure to begin a comforting and loving relationship with each individual animal over and over again every day before heading into the paddock for formal training sessions and then doing those same caretaking things again upon returning after the sessions were done.

Once that bond of trust was established, it was time for lunging to take place. When horses are lunged, they are encouraged to first walk, then trot, and finally to run around and around in a circle. The initial and primary objective of lunging is to develop communication between trainer and horse. The trainer knows this has happened when the animals begin to respond to the voice instructions being directed at them.

Even though Sally and Mateo tweaked some basic parts of the formula by altering the steps involved during the training sessions so as to match the personalities of each of their four horses, the process of lunging generally followed the same procedure: the horse would first be put in the arena and attached to what is called a lead rope. With time, patience, and consistency shown by the handler, the horse would slowly learn to respond to commands given and would begin to move in the specific direction desired by the person who was holding the rope.

Now, it's true that at this point some handlers on other ranches and farms quickly resort to the whip to get their horses to obey directions being given, but Sally and Mateo purposefully refrain from hitting their horses at all costs. Even to this day, the whip that is carried in their outstretched hand is never used for beatings, but instead serves to proffer an occasional gentle touch on the horse's backside, which helps guide and encourage the horse to move one way or the other.

During that whole process of lunging the horses, Sally and Mateo always looked for certain behaviors to evidence themselves. When they noticed these indicators, they knew that the horses were willing to accept and follow their commands. Once they saw those signs, they recognized that the horses were acknowledging it would be their handlers who would assume the role of leader during these training sessions. Some signs of acceptance they looked for would be when the horses drop their head lower than usual, shorten the circle, start licking, move with a relaxed, swinging tail or snort. As soon as any or most of these things began to happen, Sally and Mateo would quickly stop the particular horse-in-training "in their tracks" (so to speak). They would then turn and face the horse directly, gazing into its eyes. Slowly, slowly, the human would then move towards the animal, and right before the they got too close to each other, the handler would reach out and gently touch the horse. After such contact, the trainer would turn around at a 45-degree angle so that their back was to the horse and start to slowly and carefully walk away. At this point, inevitably, the animal would follow their human guide naturally and willingly. A lead rope was no longer needed after this point, as the horses readily stayed behind the person walking in front of them, willingly following them, wherever they went.

Once the horses understand and are willing to follow the handler's directions, they are taken around the arena on slow walks that gradually turn into trots and finally into runs. The practice of lunging is never really dropped and continues throughout the time the trainer and the horse are together, but most of those later sessions might only last for just a few minutes before the horse is mounted. From that point on, lunging serves to loosen up the horses before formal riding excursions but sometimes it just lets them safely burn off extra energy when they are not going to be ridden for a while. No matter if it is in the initial training or follow-up refresher exercises, it is critical that the process of lunging is always done correctly and that it be received as a positive experience. Horses who have been appropriately lunged develop both a strong sense of balance and a deep awareness of their own natural rhythms. Their overall gait improves and helps them stay strong for all the remaining years of their life. Happily, the four horses at The Palm Tree Ranch really enjoy being lunged.

All strategies that Sally and Mateo used during the early training sessions were, first and foremost, grounded in the notion of respect for the intellect, the strength and the abilities of the horses. Mateo explained this idea to one of the new ranch hands, and I couldn't have said it any better: "You have to develop mutual trust. You can't expect your horses to take care of you if you don't take care of them. It's an on-going process and you must always be kind and calm when dealing with horses. Do that, and you've built a life-long mutually loving relationship!"

Mateo doesn't just talk the talk. He truly walks the walk. Same for Sally. Same for the ranch hand manager, Gabriel. And now the same for the other ranch hands they have hired and also for all the interns and volunteers who come on a regular basis to help with the multitude of the daily chores that must be done to keep The Palm Tree Ranch thriving and successful. Since Sally and Mateo can't be everywhere at once, they have also conveyed and demonstrated to everyone the best techniques for handling their horses.

Everyone at The Ranch takes the responsibility of caring for the horses seriously. They know that the horses are truly the heart and soul of the work being done there. No newcomers balk when told that before they are allowed to work directly with the horses, they must first learn to make fluid, slow movements around the horses. They also know that they must announce their presence when walking up to the herd, which is done by calmly and at a conversational level saying the name of each of the horses. Once those behaviors are ingrained and natural, then and only then are they are allowed to go out to the pasture where the horses are grazing. Upon arriving where the herd is gathered, they should then slowly reach out, gently rub the horse's mane and make sure to thank that horse for being such an important part of the mission of The Palm Tree Ranch. This consistency in approach keeps the horses relaxed and helps prepares them to remain serene and well prepared for any and every thing once they begin working with the children who will be arriving for therapy sessions that day.

Watching the trainers and ranch hands approach the horses with love and respect is always a touching sight for me to witness, but equally wonderful is watching the horses while this is happening, for they are not just standing there passively waiting but instead are carrying out their own particular behaviors during this greeting ritual.

As soon as they hear their names being called, the horses all stop eating and turn toward the person approaching them, sometimes walking forward to greet the person, sometimes standing their ground, maybe lifting their head to nicker or whinny as a way of saying hello, maybe dropping their head onto the person's shoulder or sometimes even giving the person a gentle nudge that feels as close to a hug as possible. No matter what the particular behavior that occurs, nowadays the horses are always relaxed when they are greeted by a person coming toward them and they easily comply when asked to walk and move together with their handlers.

"Oh, yes," I heard Sally explain while on a phone call with a friend from faraway who was trying to envision life at The Palm Tree Ranch. "We are very attentive to our horses. We walk out among them every day, which helps them remember to follow our lead, stopping when we stop, running when we run, walking when we walk. We only saddle them when riding. Most of the time they wear bareback pads and feel the freedom from restraint that is so natural to horses out in the wild. They are well trained but also well cared for, that's for sure!"

Yes, indeed, well trained, but not like any other horses doing any other kind of work, because here at The Ranch the horses have to be prepared to meet and work with children who have a wide variety of special needs, which means further and more specific on-going training for the horses in this herd, well beyond lunging, is definitely needed. Because the horses must be able to not only let the children come up near them but also to remain calm while they ride on them and then to accept the hands of the child who wants to groom them during therapy sessions (even if those hands are rough or erratic), it is vitally important that these very large animals learn to keep steady and stay sure-footed no matter what happens.

To their credit, Sally and Mateo realized early on that it was critical to provide the horses with all kinds of practice sessions that would help them be ready for some unexpected and occasionally surprising actions that very well might arise once the children started coming for therapy. The goal with this part of the training was to help the horses be prepared for anything because, for sure, just about any and every thing that is possible would happen.

Sally and Mateo incorporated training techniques that would never be needed for horses who lived and worked in other settings. For example, as they walk with the horses in the ring or ride with them out in the fields, they might suddenly speak very loudly and then alternate by using soft whispers. They might start petting them all over or simply poke at them. They might also play with their tails and their manes, gently tugging on both.

Immediately after each of these unexpected—and somewhat inappropriate—behaviors, they would pause and explain to the horse, "Just getting you ready for the children." This sentence quickly became the mantra for this phase of training and they continue to use it whenever they have training sessions with the horses, even to this day.

All these techniques that Sally and Mateo developed and continue to use with the horses were designed with one goal in mind: to desensitize the horses so they would not be surprised or spooked if any wild or unexpected behaviors occurred when they were working with children. Predicting ahead of time specific behaviors that each child will exhibit is impossible, as each one comes with a set of individual needs, backgrounds and personalities, but one thing that Sally and Mateo know for sure, is that all those children will go through a variety of emotions during the equine therapy sessions. While one youngster might be angry and agitated, another might feel nervous and fearful. Some children may be uncommunicative and quiet, while some might be excited and overly-eager. And the same child who was reticent to be near the horses one week might very well shout greetings and come running toward them the next week. In order to handle the wide variety of emotions that they will surely be feeling at different times, the children might yell or screech or even latch onto the horse in an impulsive and strong manner. Those children who have autism might also attempt to fulfill a sensory need by yanking on the horse's mane during the ride.

With all those possibilities racing in their minds, Sally and Mateo knew preparing the horses for a wide variety of circumstances and conditions was essential. They are constantly designing and adapting activities to encourage and support the horses in accepting a wide variety and assortment of sounds, smells, sights, and behaviors.

Anyone watching these training sessions might easily be struck by how unconventional and unexpected the activities Sally and Mateo have devised really are, for they are nothing like those used to train horses on most other ranches. The numerous learning events that take place using hula hoops, basketballs, bubbles, toys, soft darts and even bean bags are all designed to help desensitize the horses.

In addition to all the up-close training, Sally and Mateo recognize that it is also important to prepare the horses for times when objects might appear unexpectedly seemingly from afar but landing in their line of vision. Leaves falling from trees, tumbleweeds blowing across the open field or even children tossing objects near the horses. To prepare for such possibilities, there are also times when Sally and Mateo fly kites close by, when swim noodles are strung up on wires and allowed to wave wildly in the wind, and sometimes when wide strips of plastic tarps are hung from trees, some to the side of the paths and some directly in the way, forcing the horses to nudge them with their noses so they could continue moving forward. I have even seen Sally and Mateo tie a plastic bag to the end of a stick and gently brush that against the horses, all over their bodies, including their legs and buttocks, so they won't rear up should something blowing in the wind come at them.

All this conditioning has taken lots of time and patience. At first, the horses would balk during these training sessions, but soon they learned to take everything in stride. And, amazingly, all these techniques really have helped the horses handle anything the children dish out during riding therapy sessions, which is quite a bit!

But if positive change was to happen for the children involved in these equine therapy sessions, in addition to all these wide-range preparatory training activities, Sally and Mateo knew there was one more essential step in the process that could not be overlooked. As they came to realize, it wasn't enough to just randomly pick one of the horses out of the herd to work with any given child. Instead, the real key to achieving effective therapy results would be in finding ideal matches between the horses and the children, for only then could a successful experience occur.

Matching horse to rider sounds like an easy task, but believe me, it's not. If a first pairing attempt works, then halleluiah! But if that first pairing turns out not to be successful for one reason or another, I have come to understand that this is where the "magic" (or the "miracle" depending on your point of view) really begins to happen. At that point, Sally and Mateo try out each horse in succession until they find a therapeutic match between horse and rider.

As soon as the perfect pairing is found, the path ahead finally becomes smooth and then, and only then, can positive changes begin to happen for the child being served. And it never ceases to amaze me that once a reliable and stable connection is made between animal and human, the best in both of them is brought out—the horse trusts the child with whom it is paired and vice versa. That strong bond of mutual trust means all are able to relax and focus on the healing process and in turn, the child grows stronger and ever more confident, as well.

It also always seems to happen at this very point in the process, just as it becomes easy for horse and child, that I have a really tough time with my assignment and grapple yet again with the restrictions that have been put upon me. I try my best to accept that, even with all the vast and wide-ranging knowledge I possess, the greatest limitation (as far as I am concerned) put upon me is that I am never allowed to directly interfere in any situation on Earth, even if I believe my assistance would bring about what I perceive to be a quicker and more satisfying result.

Many is the time I have heard the explanation that all creatures, great and small, must be given the chance to succeed on their own. I recognize that I am not as wise as The One Who Guides Us All, but I often think if I just had a magical wand, I could wave it and make all the problems and woes of individual beings—as well as those of the populace at large—disappear. And I really do believe that then everyone here on Earth would be forever happy.

This is where my own faith gets tested. Because I am not allowed to "fix" everything that I identify as a problem, I have to believe in the wisdom of those who reign from on high and who have the best interests in mind for all things—living and inanimate. I have to believe that good will be triumphant. I have to believe that eventually kindness will prevail for everyone. And most of all, I have to believe that someday every person will come to realize that only through cooperation, kindness, and faith in a greater good, can true harmony reign in this place they call home.

At this point, as my own sense of faith begins to flag, I am usually summoned to meet with those up above. I can't say how much time passes during these meetings, for time on Earth is calculated much differently than time among the stars, but I eventually calm down and find my way again. At that point, I am allowed to return to that Big

Blue Marble and am always amazed to find not one single Earth-day has passed since I left. I always come back with a sense of renewed purpose. Yes, I am allowed to remain at The Palm Tree Ranch because I have once again vowed to observe and am truly content with the knowledge that simply placing possibilities in front of those whom I serve, always being careful not to force my will upon them, is my own particular calling. I dig deep and find my faith that The One Who Guides Us All has a bigger and grander plan. I truly believe that justice and equity will one day arrive for everyone. After I weather one of these recurring test-of-confidence times, I marvel that my own faith has been strengthened and I am enabled just a bit more to understand the positive power and importance of the ruling doctrine which declares that it is critical humans be able to act independently from each other, even though it seems obvious to me that they are most effective when they act in concert and harmony with all living things.

Certainly, here at The Palm Tree Ranch, where belief and faith are so strong, the therapists, children and horses open passageways to healing that had never before seemed possible. Amazingly powerful connections are made between horse and child during equine therapy sessions, and each time a breakthrough occurs, Mateo and Sally can be heard to say prayers of thankfulness, which always include the phrase, "it's miraculous how they bring out the best in each other!"

I may not be able to change things just because I want them to change, but one of my powers that I certainly appreciate and that I recognize as being ever so important in my work is the ability to communicate directly with animals, with very young children, and also with those of all ages who are determined by society to be disabled in some form or another and are thus underserved, marginalized or just plain ignored. The methods of communication I employ are by no means traditional. I don't directly talk or sign with anyone, but instead we communicate by mutually picking up and responding to thoughts that are sent out into the ether.

Over the past few years, I have watched carefully to take note of all the changes that have occurred and through carefully attending to the messages sent by both horses and children, been able to gain insight and input about the process and the outcomes of these equine therapy sessions.

Focusing In

The young people who are brought to The Palm Tree Ranch for therapeutic services are usually powerless to express what would help change their own personal life circumstances. These wee ones find themselves relying on the understanding, knowledge and kindness of people around them to transport them to a place of healing.

How remarkable is the combined life experiences of all these children. However, every single child has a unique, individual tale to tell and each story is significant and momentous in its own right, but these children either cannot or do not wish to speak for themselves.

You might then ask, who shall tell these stories? Who will speak for the children? Turns out, it is me, Thou-Est. It was only after I had been assigned to The Palm Tree Ranch for several Earth years that I was blessed with this new and very specific directive from The One Who Guides Us All. At that point, in addition to continuing along with my original assignment where I was allowed to observe and gently provide insights into what could be, I was also bestowed the honor of taking on the role of narrator for events happening at The Palm Tree Ranch.

The One gave me three specific objectives for writing and publishing these tales: one of those reasons is primarily for the children themselves and the other two are not only for them but also for all those who work at The Ranch, and maybe most of all, for you, my dear readers.

First and foremost, I write to honor the powerful and righteous strength of character the children bring with them, not only to life in general but most specifically to their ongoing therapy sessions. From the outset, from the moment that the children arrive at The Palm Tree Ranch, they embark upon their journey toward healing, which will not come easily or quickly. They must dig deep for continued resolve to accept the balm being offered. Only then will the pains and woes they have endured during the very young stages of their lives be soothed with courage and strength as they face their futures.

Next, I write to serve as a reminder that—even though it may be difficult for some of us to imagine or believe—every single life brought to this Earth is equally beautiful and purposeful in the eyes of the Creator.

And finally, (but not any less important than the other two aims), I write to inspire those people who are currently physically and emotionally abled in hopes that they should offer not only an attitude of generosity toward others, but actual generosity to anyone in need. For it is only through acts of kindness and love (large and small) that positive change can and will occur, not only for those people whom they are helping but more so within their very own selves.

And, now that you have been informed that the teller of these tales will be your very humble servant, Thou-Est, you might ask, how will these stories be written?

Tenderly. Very tenderly and with much love.

Respect and honor will be paid to everyone involved in each of these vignettes. Now, before I begin regaling you with these tales, I must make clear one condition that was ordered by The One and will be followed with great care, which is that there will be much caution and restraint made in the telling of these stories, as the right to privacy for everyone involved must be carefully guarded. Alas, over all the numerous years I have been around humans, I have witnessed too many occasions where demand to know all the minutiae of another person's life becomes overwhelmingly strong. Too often once those details are shared, they are not treasured by the ones who learn them and instead, too easily and far too sadly, become fodder for gossip, ridicule, scorn, or even what might pass as comedy in some circles.

Oh, people. If we all only abided by the principle that human life must always be afforded dignity, wouldn't the world be a better place?

Unfortunately, I have borne direct witness over the years to the hurt felt by those involved in quite a few real-life stories when their tales were improperly appropriated by another. I know full well that whether the resulting emotional pain and injury was purposeful or accidental, it still hurts. So, it is with much carefulness and restraint that I have worded these tales. No apprehensions, though, as you should easily be able to become invested in these life stories. All of these disclaimers merely mean that, contrary to what you might desire, I know there is no need for every single detail from the lives of these children to be exposed. I can assure you with the utmost confidence that none of the basic, critical facts will be missing and that these stories will feel vibrant and complete.

Oh, and there is just one more thing I need to discuss with you before I begin my telling of the tales of children and their equine therapeutic sessions. In order to truly understand the dynamics of this kind of physical therapy, it would surely help if I provided just a bit more context, which I can do by harkening back to the titular part of the equation in equine therapy: the horses.

The family tree of today's horses actually began long ago with a very tiny member of the species that would one day 'grow up" to become the size of modern horses. As far back as scientists on this planet can possibly take us when investigating that family chain, which is as much as 10 million years ago, we are aware that these noble beasts journeyed all over this planet. When this particular animal first appeared upon this Earth, its main mission and purpose in life was not to serve the needs or wants of humans but instead to roam free and untethered all across the lands where they were born. And then about 6,000 years ago, in the steppes of southern Russia and Kazakhstan, the capture and domestication of horses first began. And since that time, people all over the world have followed the practice of "reining in" horses to serve their own particular needs. Over the centuries, horses have been used in both war and peace-time settings for hunting, for sport, for conveyance, and now for healing. And, over time, horses and humans have become so ingrained in a shared history that it is now difficult to imagine one without the other.

What specifically is it about this particular animal that first drew and continues to draw the attention of humans and to fill them with the urge to bond with horses? The simple explanation is that people quickly found these noble beasts to be strong, resilient, and above all, extremely interactive animals. They quickly envisioned that domesticating these animals could provide the means to more proficiently expand their own territories. Not only that, but they also saw that horses would help them engage in highly profitable, longer-reaching trade practices and, I add somewhat sadly for all of humanity, help them wage war against one another in what they considered to be a more efficient and powerful manner.

As for me, it has been so interesting to watch the whole process evolve and I am everlastingly grateful that I've been privy to witness it all. And, oh my goodness, it is so amazing to think about the multitude of changes horses have experienced over the course of many generations! To have begun my observations so long ago means that I got to first watch them meander along their own chosen paths, grazing on wild grass, shrubs and plants, drinking from springs, brooks or lakes, basking in the sun or resting in the shade. I enjoyed that time of observing so much, mainly because the rhythm and flow of their lives always seemed natural and uncomplicated. And then I witnessed the rapid changes when humans decided they would use these particular animals for their own purposes. Of course, at first the horses rebelled against being captured and railed against being housed in barn stalls, but over several generations, tamed horses slowly evolved to not only accept being domesticated but to somehow embrace the symbiotic relationship that developed between humans and themselves.

Even though horses are not able to speak the same language as humans, they have nonetheless developed very predictable and reliable methods of expressing their feelings to people with whom they interact. Now, I find it to be a truly wonderful thing, that horses have figured out ways to communicate their own thoughts and feelings to the humans hanging around them!

Of course, there are some people who ignore the non-verbal signals horses send out and they end up either clashing or feeling no connection with these noble animals. But for those people who tune into the behaviors of horses, who approach them calmly and with respect, ah, then they are able to figure out if the animals are angry, scared, upset, hurt, anxious, or content and willing to work together with their human owners. When horses are relaxed and content, they lower their heads, shift their ears to face forward, and move their mouths in a "licking and chewing" manner. These are some of the ways they indicate that all is well with the world. However, when they sense danger or something out of the ordinary, if they smell something unusual, or if the other horses around them get alerted, everything about the horses in a herd changes. Their heads come up, their ears perk up and point in the direction of the threat. At this moment, the horses may run, snort, whinny, or kick. They are ready and willing to defend themselves, but first they warn everyone around them of this intention by sending out clear-cut signals based on the way their ears are positioned. For example, when horses pin their ears back far enough to touch their own heads, stand clear, for it means they are about to kick, buck or run.

While some adults have the gift of successfully understanding messages being sent by horses, it is the children of this world who, as a group, tend to be more in tune to the ways of the horse. Even for children who have never before directly come into contact with any horses, once they encounter such an animal the potential for connection is electric and charged and ready to occur. And more often than not, once a strong and positive connection has been firmly established, only good things will follow.

But for horses and humans (adults and children alike) to develop trust in one other, it takes more than just understanding the non-verbal messages each is sending out. More than that, they must truly care about each other, for then, and only then, can they begin to help each other become the best version of themselves. And this is going to takes time, patience and above all, faith.

Now, back to the stories I am about to tell. Even though I would prefer to relate the individual accounts of every single child who has ever come to The Palm Tree Ranch, and yes, there has been such a great number, I have been directed to choose and recount only a few tales. In these stories, not only will you learn about the path these children have taken, but also of the journey that their parents/guardians/caretakers who are inextricably connected to these children have embarked upon as well.

Please remember that these stories are meant to serve as exemplars; therefore, not one of the changes I have made should in any way diminish or alter your appreciation for the positive results that have consistently been produced through the equine therapy sessions offered at The Palm Tree Ranch.

While it is true that singular efforts can yield a certain measure of success in anything that is done at The Palm Tree Ranch, it quickly becomes obvious to all who come and spend time at this blessed place that the knowledge, faith and love emanating from each therapist, each horse, each child, and each parent/guardian/caretaker somehow miraculously combines together and enables the potential for success to become greater and stronger than any one separated, distinct source could possibly generate.

And now, with all my clarifications, elucidations and caveats explained, I offer the following three vignettes of healing and hope that have occurred at The Palm Tree Ranch over the past few years, witnessed to and ascribed by yours truly.

Alberto: Finding Peace

Sally and Mateo learned about Alberto's history well before he first arrived at The Palm Tree Ranch. This young child had surely lived through so much trauma and pain in his brief life here on Earth that it might have been too much for anyone even five times his age to bear, yet here he was, having endured. Bent but not broken. Quite an accomplishment for anyone, but most impressive because Alberto was only eight years old.

His life story wasn't fair or right. But it was the way it was. Once authorities discovered what Alberto was going through, the decision to offer therapy was obvious as a way to help him cope with the harsh treatment he had received over the past years, so vile and horrific, from the one person he should have been able to trust the most: his own parent.

Growing up in a house where he was physically beaten by his father on regular occasions for the slightest infraction—and sometimes for no reason whatsoever—Alberto learned to hold his anger in check when at home, but whenever he left that setting, be it on the streets or in the school building, he hurled his own form of vengeance on anyone who dared to cross his path.

"It's really so sad," Sally remarked to the school official recommending Alberto for equine therapy. "To be only eight years old and to be so very hurt inside that you want to cause damage to any and every one you meet in the world."

The school social worker agreed and added, "It really is sad. But as soon as we found out about the conditions at his home, we had him removed and placed in foster care. His mother is currently trying to get him back, but first she has to move out of that house away from Alberto's abusive father and then she needs to demonstrate that she can financially support both herself and her child. I hear she is getting assistance from her church and we are all hoping that she can turn things around."

Sally made a sound as if to talk, but words failed her, so she merely nodded.

The social worker continued, "For now, though, we at the school are trying to deal with ways to control Alberto's temper outbursts by helping him find alternative solutions to deal with his anger. We've used various approaches to get him to calm down when he starts to get upset and have tried to help him understand that when he beats on another person, the pain he is inflicting is the same kind of pain his father caused him when they were living together."

Again, Sally tried to comment and once again, words failed her.

Sally put her hand to her heart, sighed deeply and focused on the social worker as the woman continued, "So far, none of our methods have worked; Alberto continues to lash out toward others in harmful ways. He still holds onto so many painful feelings about his own mistreatment and abuse that one day we fear he won't be able to control his built-up rage and if that happens, he might seriously injure another student or a teacher. We want him to stay in the school system, but for the safety of himself and all around him, we are rapidly nearing the end of what we can tolerate. So, we came to you as a last resort."

Mateo picked up the file with Alberto's name on it and opened it. He had already read it through, cover to cover, dozens of times and knew most of it by heart, but somehow holding the file with the dreadful pictures of Alberto's shattered and contorted body after he had endured that final beating from his father pained his heart as if he were seeing it for the first time.

Sally and Mateo looked at each other and then, in unison, turned to the social worker and said, "Bring him to The Ranch. We will see what healing our horses can bring for Alberto."

And so, Alberto arrived. As Sally saw the car coming down the driveway, she handed the reins of Bella over to Gabriel and slowly walked out of the paddock and toward the vehicle. Alberto didn't even look up at her but stayed slumped down in the back seat, arms crossed and an angry look on his face. Mateo stood nearby in case he needed to intervene should Alberto attack Sally or one of the horses. He made sure to be mostly out of sight, though, for he figured the last thing Alberto needed was to see a 6-foot man looming over him and he certainly didn't want in any way to intimidate the young boy, especially as Sally was going to have a hard enough time trying to gain the lad's trust.

"Go on, Alberto" said the school social worker from the front passenger seat, "go on. We came here for you so you need to get out of the car and go meet Sally. Just like I told you on the ride here, Sally will take care of you on your visits to this ranch. She's the one who will teach you how to ride a horse."

Alberto said nothing in reply but instead hunched even lower in the seat, casting his eyes further downward. He crossed his arms in a defiant posture and refused to open the car door.

Sally stood patiently next to the automobile. Mateo moved even a bit further back and dropped down behind a huge bale of hay so that he was almost out of sight should Alberto look up to check out the surroundings. Bella stood her ground inside the paddock, looking over the fence toward the automobile but making no movements or sounds as she, too, waited and watched.

Sally leaned down so her face would show through the back window of the car and began talking, softly and slowly, "Hello, Alberto. It is nice to meet you and to have you here visiting us today. Even though we have several horses here at The Palm Tree Ranch, we chose

Bella as the horse for you to meet first. As you can see, not only is she big and beautiful, but she has a very calm nature and loves being ridden."

Alberto continued averting his eyes but Sally figured that he was listening to everything she was saying, and so she continued, "Bella is actually a mother to many horses. Turns out that all of them live at the ranch right next door to us. I don't think she misses them too much though, because we make sure that she gets to see her babies whenever we take her out on the trail for rides. And she really does like being ridden, but you first have to get to know each other. So, when you are ready, you should come out of the car and walk up to her quietly. Let her meet you in her own way. Treat her calmly and try to show her some love. If you do, very soon the two of you will be good friends. But I've got to warn you that just like all horses, if you come at Bella angry or too quickly, she will react, and not in a good way."

Sally stopped talking and stood up, waiting perfectly still to see if her message was getting through. She held her breath, watching carefully to see if Alberto would look up or respond in any way to all that she had said. As soon as she saw him move just a bit and then, inch by inch slide his hand across the seat of the car toward the latch and when he finally pulled up on it, opening the door, she knew they were making progress. And then slowly, ever so slowly, Alberto swung first one leg and then the other onto the ground and hoisted himself up and out of the car. He made no eye contact with Sally, but instead of staring at the ground, he raised his head and began looking all around him. His brow was furrowed and a serious frown was frozen on his face. He was taking in every single thing within his view but still he said nothing.

Now I want you to remember, just like all the other humans there that day, Alberto had no consciousness of my presence and had no knowledge that I, Thou-Est, existed on a whole different plane than all beings living on this planet. Ironically, it was precisely because of this disconnection-connection that I was able to bond with Alberto. Of course, the young boy overtly remained oblivious to my presence but the cosmic link between us allowed me to understand his feelings. He looked angry but as I read his innermost thoughts, I learned that he was in fact not so much angry but instead was hiding the fear and worry that he was experiencing, especially as it related to his deep-seated distrust of all adults.

Despite everything the social worker had told him about how he was chosen specially to participate in this program at The Palm Tree Ranch and how wonderful it would be for him to learn how to ride horses, Alberto wasn't sure why he had been singled out from all the other students in his class. Even though he couldn't remember anything bad he had done just before she called him down to her office, he figured he was in trouble. Truth is, even though he never said anything to the social worker, Alberto didn't want to learn how to ride horses. He didn't want to go to some ranch that was probably located far away from his school. He didn't really even want to be in school, either. But now that he no longer lived with his parents, he figured he had to do what that social worker lady told him to do or else he worried that she would send him far away and he missed his mother so much that he couldn't imagine never seeing her ever again.

In the blink of an eye, I was able to tap into Alberto's memory of that meeting at school and all that he was thinking and feeling. Even though I couldn't reach out to him directly, I could guide him as he processed what he was experiencing. I was able to highlight some of the surrounding details, which would give him the opportunity to appreciate all that he was seeing. It might have seemed like a long time was passing to the adults waiting for Alberto to say or do something, but it was actually only a moment or two as he stood next to the car, taking in the whole of the scene around him, noticing the trails leading off into the fields, the nearby stable, the outbuildings on one side and the farm house set off on the other side of the paddock. His gaze then moved down to the ground but right back up as he felt the need to sweep his eyes all around him once again. He finally landed and stayed on Bella. Alberto was taken aback at the sight of her because, while he had seen plenty of pictures of horses, until this day he had never seen a live one and certainly not one this close up.

Alberto continued to stand in that same spot, almost frozen in his tracks but the furrow on his brow smoothed out and his mouth relaxed into a more neutral appearance. He tilted his head as he kept staring at Bella. Alberto was surprised at how big this horse was, even compared to that adult named Sally. Alberto was a little bit thankful for her being there since she didn't look worried at all about how big that horse was. And he was really thankful for the buffer of the car and of the fence, both of which came between him and this huge animal. Looking directly at Bella got to be a bit too much for Alberto, and he sure didn't want to look at Sally standing there next to him and he felt the same about the social worker sitting in the car so he shifted his gaze somewhat downward. That's when Alberto had a chance to see a different angle of that big horse, as he took a long and hard look at Bella's legs and hooves. They seemed gigantic to the young boy and caused him to blink a few times to be sure he was seeing what he thought he was seeing. And then slowly, ever so slowly, his eyes moved upward until he had yet another clear view of the whole of Bella. Without even knowing it, Alberto gasped as he took in the immense height and strength of that majestic animal.

Sally looked at Alberto and quietly said, "Bella is big, isn't she? But the wonderful thing is that she doesn't use her size to intimidate or hurt others. You couldn't find a kinder, more gentle horse no matter how hard you tried."

Alberto did not say anything but just kept staring at Bella, who now returned the boy's gaze by staring directly at him. To Sally and even to Mateo from his distant vantage point, it was clear that Bella was sizing up this little child. They were sure that Bella had noticed the scowl he had on his face when he got out of the car and even though he didn't look angry any more, she was more than likely picking up on the young boy's propensity to be aggressive. Generally peaceful and relaxed around children, Bella instead seemed wary and on guard this time.

The tension in the air between this young child and this horse was surprisingly strong and palpable. Sally walked slowly and calmly toward Bella, reached into her pocket for a piece of a carrot, placed it in the palm of her hand and held it out over the fence post so the horse could take the treat, connect with her owner and hopefully relax a bit. Bella moved forward for the treat and reacted as she always did when spending time with Sally, offering sweet nuzzling and soft neighing while Sally stroked her mane, saying loud enough for the young boy to hear, "You are such a beauty, Bella. I'm looking forward to you getting to meet a new visitor. His name is Alberto and I hope the two of you will get to be great friends."

Alberto looked away for a moment when he first saw Sally move toward Bella, then turned back to watch what was happening. When he heard what Sally said to the horse, Alberto just grunted a bit in scorn and shook his head back and forth. That was his way of saying that it was almost too much to absorb. He appeared even more angry than ever and virtually oozed ill feelings toward one and all.

There was definitely a feeling of rage coming from Alberto, but it was mingled with a sense of confusion and bafflement. He still couldn't figure out why he had been brought to this particular ranch, he couldn't understand why this woman would be nuzzling that enormous horse, and he felt intense fear that he might be required to directly interact with this beast of an animal.

I was keenly aware of all of this, but as usual, I was powerless to alter any of Alberto's feelings or offer any explanation directly to the young boy. My lot, I reminded myself, was to offer silent support and observe what transpired. And so, I watched.

Sally spoke softly and slowly to Alberto, all the while rubbing Bella's forelock. "See how gentle Bella is, Alberto. She really likes to be groomed. That's something you will learn to do over time, but for now, you need to introduce yourself to her. When you're ready, just calmly walk over here and put this carrot in your flattened palm then slowly reach out your hand toward her, like I just did. She will greet you with the same energy that you put into that gesture. Try your best to move calmly and carefully."

Alberto stood his ground for a few moments. Then he shook his head, grunted again, and hastily strode right up to the fence. "I'm not afraid of you, horse," he thought to himself. "I'm not afraid of anything." With those thoughts in his mind, he elbowed Sally aside. He didn't take the carrot she offered but instead just stuck his hand out quickly and with a great deal of force, placing it directly into Bella's face.

And then Bella, did something she had never done in all the time since she started working with the children coming to The Palm Tree Ranch: she lunged out and attempted to bite Alberto's hand!

Sally saw it all happening as if in slow motion, which actually gave her time to read the situation and react before Alberto's hand ended up in Bella's mouth. Sally came up behind Alberto and gently put her hands on his shoulders, pulling him back away from the horse.

Alberto let out a yell and a curse and started to move forward, his right hand balled up into a fist. "I'm gonna kill that horse for trying to hurt me!" he thought to himself.

Sally still held onto his shoulders and momentarily Alberto was unable to go anywhere. Gabriel quickly guided Bella back away from the fence. The social worker wondered if she should interfere, but instead stayed in the car once she realized that Sally had the situation in hand. Mateo, who was still watching from behind the haystack, started to step out of the shadows, ready to offer assistance in subduing the boy if necessary. He quickly saw that Sally had everything under control and so, before his presence was noted, he quietly moved back behind the bales of hay once more.

Despite Alberto's fury and strength, Sally's determination to protect the young boy was even greater. She held onto him for a moment, told him to breathe and relax, then let go of his shoulders. At that point, she moved to stand between the little child and the huge horse behind the fence, turned and kneeled down so she could look directly at the child's face.

"Wow. First time for everything," Sally told Alberto. "Bella has never done anything like that before. Remember what I told you earlier, that horses can sense how people are feeling and what they are thinking. Bella felt all that negative energy you were sending out. It wasn't that she wanted to hurt you but instead she was just protecting herself. Try to remember the Golden Rule which tells us that we should treat others the way we want to be treated. What that means, Alberto, is that if you want Bella to be kind to you, then you should be kind to her."

Alberto stood perfectly still while Sally was talking to him. I could sense that he was quite shaken up and a bit shocked that such a large animal could turn on him so quickly. He also recognized that he was partly to blame for what had just happened.

For the first time that day, Alberto spoke, "That horse scared me!"

Sally nodded in understanding as she responded, "I think that horse was scared, too."

Alberto took a moment to absorb what he was hearing, then said, "I just wanted to show her who was boss. Figured it was better to act tough so she'd be scared of me. But it sure didn't work out the way I thought it would."

Sally smiled and said, "I think you'll quickly learn that horses have their own minds and ways of doing things. Our job isn't to hurt them until they submit to our will, but instead to find ways that we can work together."

"Do I have to try to work together any more today?" asked Alberto.

Sally laughed and said, "No. Let's just say that lesson one is done."

Alberto breathed a sigh of relief and his body relaxed just a bit.

Sally stayed exactly where she was, safely between the boy and the horse. She stayed lowered and looked directly into Alberto's eyes as she continued, "You'll be coming back to see us again in two days. Until then, think about how what you do not only impacts you but also all the others around you. Think about how Bella picked up on your anger so quickly. The next time you come, try to be more relaxed and ready to work with her because if the same thing happens again, if you come at her too quickly and with the kind of anger you put out today, you better be ready, for she'll react to your behavior exactly like she just did, for sure!"

Alberto crossed his arms but made no attempt to move away, as Sally added, "One thing we hope you come to understand during your time here at The Ranch is that we know you have lots of reasons to be angry at the world, but we believe you also have reasons to be grateful, too. When you constantly vent your own bottled-up anger toward others it may feel good at first, but it not only hurts them, in the long run it also hurts you, too. Over the next couple of days, when those strong feelings of anger wash over you, maybe you could stop for a moment, close your eyes and take a deep breath. When you open your eyes, try to think about one thing, no matter how small, that makes you feel happy. And then when you come back here to The Palm Tree Ranch, we can talk about how you did controlling your anger."

I tuned into Alberto's thoughts while Sally was talking. I sent him waves of my own positive energy to help him absorb the message. Can't change what he does, but I can help him envision all the alternate paths available to him. He heard her words, but I knew he didn't totally understand what she meant.

Yet.

Alberto's face took on a puzzled look as he tried to absorb all of Sally's message. "Wait," said Alberto. "You mean I really do have to come back again? Even after what just happened with that horse? I don't like it here. Please. Please. From now on, I'll be good at school. I really will. I promise. I'll do whatever the teacher says to do and I won't beat up anyone, even if they deserve it!"

At this point, the school social worker got out of the car and walked over closer to where Alberto was standing, telling him, "That's great news, Alberto. I'm glad you're ready to do your best at school. It's wonderful to hear you say you'll stop bullying and hurting the other students. But we all think coming here for a while will do you a lot of good. You'll have a chance to spend time being around this beautiful horse and someday if you're fortunate enough, you might be allowed to get up and ride on her. Your goal of not hurting the other students starting right now is a good goal and I hope you can make it come true. But even so, you will be coming back here in two days and then twice every week for the foreseeable future."

Alberto said nothing but just turned his head a bit to look out into the distance.

Sally added, "Alberto, please don't think of your time here at The Ranch as punishment. I'm so glad we got to meet you. It's a joy to have you visit here and soon you might discover that you really like being around all of our sweet and wonderful horses. But for now, let's leave Bella in the arena while we take a tour of the place. That way you can get to know where everything is located. Before we do that, though, there is someone I want you to meet. Don't worry, it's not another horse! It's my husband, Mateo, who also works here at The Palm Tree Ranch."

At that point, Mateo slowly moved out from behind the hay bales so he could be seen. He walked over to where everyone was standing. Sally introduced him to Alberto and after Mateo greeted the young boy, he turned, opened the gate and walked into the paddock, shutting the gate behind him.

Sally said, "Mateo is going to help Gabriel take care of Bella now." And with that, Sally and Alberto went to take a tour of the place. When they arrived back at the paddock, Alberto looked over at Bella one more time, said good-bye to Sally, got in the car and returned to school. End of session one. But, as promised, not the last session.

Despite his initial worries and reluctance to participate in the equine therapy program designed for him, Alberto was brought back to The Ranch twice a week for months and months. Surprisingly, Alberto's behavior began to change in quite a dramatic fashion even by his second visit. Instead of sitting slumped in the back seat, he got out of the car without needing any encouragement at all. He and Sally walked up calmly toward the paddock and Alberto asked her for a carrot. He then gently reached out his hand, holding out the carrot as a greeting. Bella came over to the fence and Alberto was amazed that what Sally had told him came true. He was calm and relaxed, and Bella seemed calm and relaxed, too. Within the very second visit to The Palm Tree Ranch, Alberto literally had Bella eating out of the palm of his hand. He totally enjoyed holding his closed hand, turning it over to reveal a carrot waiting there for the horse to take from him. Because he held his hand steady, Bella happily accepted the treat the boy was offering.

You might wonder: how could this be true? How could such a quick turnaround between the young boy and the older horse happen? Well, before getting out of the car on that second visit, I noticed that Alberto was practicing using the breathing technique that Sally had suggested. Drawing in long, slow breaths and fully exhaling helped to make him feel a bit more relaxed and most amazingly of all, he was able to call up a loving memory to help him stay calm. He thought about how his mother's hugs felt and he closed his eyes for just a moment, feeling grateful to have that memory. And from that very moment, Alberto started to believe that he didn't have to hurt that big horse anymore. As for Bella, well, she was quick to sense the change for the better in Alberto's attitude and, exactly as Sally had predicted, responded in kind.

Over time, each successful visit brought Alberto and Bella even closer.

At first, Alberto was content to enjoy spending time with Bella from the safety of standing outside the fence, but it wasn't too many sessions later that he willingly went into the arena and got to meet Bella up close. As soon as he was able to calmly stand near the horse, Sally began teaching him the steps needed to properly groom a horse. Once he mastered the art of taking care of Bella's physical needs, he was given the reins so he could lead her around, walking in large circles within the paddock. And finally, one day, when both were ready, Alberto was hoisted up on Bella's back. He learned to ride her within the fenced area and much later he was then allowed to go out on chaperoned trail rides.

And much, much later, came a day that was spent first grooming Bella and then taking her on a most successful ride around the arena. Sally and Mateo walked over to chat with Alberto as he came down off of the horse's back. Alberto handed the reins over to Mateo and ran right up to Sally, giving her a huge hug. "Hey, thanks for letting me come to The Ranch! I love being near horses now. Maybe I might work with them when I grow up. Bella and me are good buddies now. I'm not scared of her and she's not scared of me. We're pals. I'm so glad I get to come here!"

Sally smiled and looked at Alberto for a moment, then said, "Funny you should say all that. I noticed how happy you seem now and how much you have grown and changed since you started coming here last year. What you say you feel about horses is so obvious. You're always kind and loving toward Bella and even the other horses in our herd come up to greet you now each time you get out of the car. That's wonderful. And lately I've been hearing great things about how you are with your fellow students in school, too."

"Yeah! I don't punch anybody anymore. And you know what's really weird? I don't even think about punching them, either!"

Upon hearing that, Sally said, "I'm so proud of you, Alberto. You really have changed so much in your time here. And all your changes have been for the better, that's for sure."

Alberto smiled at Sally, and though she was feeling such mixed emotions, she knew the moment had come when she had to say the most wonderful but also at the same time the hardest thing she ever had to say when working with at-risk children. She reached out and took his hand as she began this part of what she planned to say. The two of them started slowly walking down the path next to the barn. "Now, Alberto, as I have been telling you for the past few weeks, it's a fact of life that all things must eventually come to an end. You've been coming here to The Palm Tree Ranch for a while now and oh, we're so proud of the progress you've made during your time here with us! Believe me, we love having you here and so does Bella. I remember that first day when Bella almost bit you. You started out furious at the world and now it's clear that you are at peace with your environment. You needed to be here then, but you don't need to be here any longer; it's time for you to move on. It's not that we wouldn't want to continue working with you, because we really would. Of course, we will miss you very much but we are excited that you have learned how to handle your emotions."

Alberto said nothing. He looked straight ahead and kept walking forward, holding tightly onto Sally's hand, waiting to hear the rest of what she had to say.

"And now, here we are, at the end of your time with us. Today will be your final session. We really do wish you could stay with us, Alberto. We wish we could continue working with you forever, but as you know, there are so many other children out there with needs just as great as yours was when you first came here."

Sally paused for a moment, looking directly at Alberto, who continued to stare straight in front of him. Then she continued, "Those children are waiting their turns, and they need our help. And unfortunately, we only have so much time on our schedule! You're one of the lucky ones. You got to come here. But you were more than lucky—you were smart, too. You used your time with us wisely and made great choices that all led you to how well you're doing now. You are what we call one of our 'graduates' which means that even though we won't see you on a regular basis, you will always remain in our thoughts, in our prayers and in our hearts, each and every day."

Alberto stopped walking, tightening his hold on Sally's hand, "Okay, truth?" He took a deep breath and let it out slowly, loosened his grip just a bit, then said, "I sure will miss coming here, but it's a good thing, isn't it? Like you said, it means I don't have that anger in my heart anymore. I like the way I am now way better than when I was mad at everyone and everything. And don't worry. Even though I'm leaving, I know I'm still gonna be okay wherever I go. I know it's fair and it's only right. I bet you already have the next angry kid lined up ready to come here to take my place. And I know he needs to be here now more than I do. Just make sure that Bella doesn't really bite that next kid's hand, though!"

And with that, Sally and Alberto started chuckling, which quickly turned into joyous whoops of laughter and shifted into a tearful but happy goodbye hug and finally finished with a trip over to share that hug with Bella.

Alberto took his place in the car, sitting bolt upright in the back seat while the social worker steered the car down the long driveway. Alberto turned, looked back at where Sally and Mateo were standing next to Bella, and waved goodbye. The car headed out of the driveway and down the road, out of sight, but of course, for everyone there at The Palm Tree Ranch, Alberto was never out of mind.

The social worker kept in touch with Sally and Mateo. How happy they all were when she shared the good news that Alberto and his mother were reunited. And then, years later, Sally and Mateo were delighted to be invited to the graduation ceremony where Alberto received his high school diploma. The young boy who carried the physical scars laid on him by an abusive father no longer carried anger in his heart. Alberto had grown into a kind and loving man, ready to head out into the world to find his own fortune.

As soon as the ceremony ended, diploma in hand, Alberto ran up to them in the audience. He hugged his mother first, then turned to thank Sally and Mateo for all they had done for him so many years ago. They reminded him that he had done most of the work on his path to healing. "Well," said Sally, "you and a friend, of course." That's when they revealed the graduation gift Mateo was holding behind his back. Alberto tore off the wrapping paper to reveal a photo that had been taken of him, years ago, sitting atop Bella shortly before that first "graduation" from The Palm Tree Ranch when he no longer needed to continue with his equine therapy sessions. The mature young man standing in front of them shed a tear, hugged the photo to his chest and declared it was the best gift he had ever received.

Aurora: One Step at a Time

E very person who ever first tried to conceive, then to bring to life, and finally to raise a child knows that ultimately it is the biggest gamble possible.

In Las Vegas, as I understand it, the phrase "the house always wins" means that no matter how hard you try your luck at the various games of chance offered at the casino, hoping to come out of it victorious so you can perhaps become a millionaire (or more), odds are that you will eventually walk away from the table with nothing but lint in your pockets.

In my universe, the phrase "nothing is guaranteed" reigns supreme, which serves to remind us that even though people might feel the heavens above owe them a good and happy life, there are no promises of an easy path to get there. The One Who Guides Us All often tells me that, for humans, the critical thing isn't what happens to them (which—contrary to the opinion of some people—is not micromanaged) but instead it's how they deal with what happens.

And with those two catchphrases in mind, I am here to tell the tale of the birth and life of a dear, sweet baby girl named Aurora. On second thought, I will begin this story even before Aurora was born so that I can set the stage for her arrival.

From the moment that Aurora's parents, Sofia and José, found out they were pregnant, they felt extra blessings each and every day and always thanked the Lord above and their lucky stars for their soon-to-be-born baby. They so wanted to have a child who would become a part of their family. From the early stages of pregnancy until the moment of birth, over all those months, they would look at each other every morning and every evening and one or the other would inevitably say, "A baby! Our baby! I can't wait to meet and get to hold our beautiful baby!"

Ah, dear humans. There is yet another saying you are often heard uttering: "Be careful what you wish for" and in this case, that wish of "I can't wait" came all too true all too soon. Turns out that Sofia and José did not have to wait the full nine months for their dear daughter to be born. The average normal pregnancy ranges from 38-40 weeks, but Aurora opted not to be average and far too early and far too fragile, she came into this world at 5:35 PM after only 26 weeks growing time inside of her mother. The doctor told Sophia and José that if their daughter had been born even two weeks earlier, she would basically have had no chance of survival. But at this stage, there was just a little bit of hope that this very small baby would live, though only time and lots of intense medical attention were needed to know for sure if that little bit of hope could turn out to be true.

As much as they longed for it, neither Sofia nor José were given the opportunity to hold their new child because as soon as Aurora was delivered into this world, she was immediately whisked to the hospital's Neonatal Intensive Care Unit (NICU). Good thing, too, for even though her lungs had grown enough to develop those little air sacs called alveoli, this baby, so small that she fit in the palm of the hand of the doctor who delivered her, was too little to breathe on her own. Into an incubator she was placed where she immediately was poked and prodded with wires and tubes, all designed to help her get the oxygen she needed and to bring her sustenance until she could both breathe and eat on her own.

Talk about odds.

Right from the outset, the doctors focused on the attention to Aurora's physical situation so this tiny little infant could flourish and grow. Because only 80% of all babies born so early survived, the medical staff continually reminded Sofia and José that it was still touch and go, and only time would tell if Aurora would eventually be able to breathe on her own. Not knowing if their dear daughter would live was painful beyond words, especially because they had no control over her medical treatment. Leaving their trust in the doctors tending to their dear daughter, her parents spent their time sending boundless and continual prayers up to the Heavens.

Interestingly, though, instead of begging or bargaining with their Maker, most of the prayers that Sofia and José said were prayers of thanksgiving for having been blessed with their own dear Aurora. It was those very deep, faith-filled feelings of having been given the greatest gift possible that helped to sustain Sofia and José as they faced the almost overwhelming challenges which came during the next few months as they visited the hospital daily. Slowly, ever so slowly, Aurora grew longer and stronger until one day she finally began to breathe on her own and then, at a much later date, she was finally able to take in food through her mouth instead of relying on being fed through a tube. Sofia and José witnessed all these developments and each day before they would head home, they said yet another prayer of thanks and, together, declared Aurora perfect. And she was perfect in their eyes and would always be so, for parents view their children through quite a different lens than anyone else on this planet, and most certainly, much differently than that of the medical community.

It was during this time of growing and developing in the NICU that the doctors discovered that this particular child, truly a survivor, was also in the 10% category of early-birth babies who have severe disabilities. In Aurora's case, she was first diagnosed with cerebral palsy and later found to also have attention deficit disorder and sensory integration disorder. The doctors explained to Sofia and José that even though Aurora might face a wide range of physical difficulties, behavioral problems, and feelings of anxiety, none of the tests indicated that there was any damage to her intellect. This news came as quite a relief to her parents. They understood that physical therapy and orthotics would help Aurora as she learned to talk and to walk and that adaptive equipment would be needed to help her accomplish academic skills such as reading and writing so that she could be successful in school. They recognized that many challenges awaited them upon Aurora's eventual arrival home.

And, after many long months of praying, hoping, anticipating and preparing, Sophia and José were finally able to bring Aurora home from the hospital, where those challenges they had predicted quickly became evident as the responsibility for helping her learn about and adjust to all the demands of living was placed primarily on their own shoulders. Days turned into weeks and weeks into months. Soon, several years had passed. Even though Sophia and José were loving and caring parents doing their best to meet Aurora's needs, clearly their efforts were not enough to provide all the care and support that their baby daughter required. Help was desperately needed.

Four long years of trying to get Aurora to be less distracted and more focused. Four long years of trying different fabrics so she would feel comfortable when wearing clothing. Four long years of moderating levels of sound and light so Aurora would be at ease and not panic because she perceived the environment around her was too intensely loud or bright. Four long years of making sure she was able to get around on her own and didn't bump into walls as she first learned to crawl and then later as she learned to walk.

Every single day during those early years of Aurora's life, Sophia and José stayed vigilant and maintained a level of "high alert" but after four years, the demands being placed on them for taking care of Aurora were slowly and surely beginning to evidence themselves in not so positive ways. They both admitted to feeling fear, worry and a general sense of helplessness when they saw that Aurora wasn't making the same strides as other children her age.

Even though they were able to share their concerns about Aurora's future, they found themselves incapable of sharing their innermost feelings and emotions. Sometimes when people cannot discuss their feelings openly, the mind and body will find ways to let the world know something is off kilter. Sophia and José each felt guilt and grief over Aurora's condition, but because they didn't talk about these thoughts, they ended up isolated from each other and from the world at large. Although they were always patient and loving when they were around Aurora, the stress of holding in their feelings was evidencing itself in other ways.

José had become very impatient with others outside of the home, displaying fits of anger at cashiers in stores if he felt they weren't ringing up his items fast enough or lambasting one of his colleagues at work if he felt they didn't complete a given task in a timely fashion.

As for Sophia, well, she suffered from intense sporadic back spasms that left her writhing in pain for days on end and also suffered from wild and erratic mood swings, often crying over seemingly minor things or sometimes laughing too loudly and too long over things that others would perceive as tragic.

After four years of taking Aurora to one medical appointment after another and meticulously following orders they were given at each of those appointments, their family doctor finally turned to Sophia and José one day and said, "You are both wonderful parents. It's clear you are doing all you can for Aurora and I can see that she is making a bit of progress. But honestly, you both look exhausted."

Aurora started fussing. Sophia held her breath while she tried to stretch the pain out of her back and José began to tap his toes in frustration, but neither of them said a word.

The doctor noted it all, waited for a few moments, then persisted, "Parents can't be expected to be able to do everything for their children, especially children who have exacting and special needs. There is a place I know that offers assistance to parents and children who are in the same circumstances as you. This place provides physical and occupational therapy, educational foundations, and life-skills development. Their work has brought about positive changes for many of the children with whom they work and I think Aurora would benefit from being there. Not only that, but they also offer respite care for parents, which is pretty clear you both need at this point."

Sophia quickly asked, "Does she have to live there? I couldn't leave her there!"

"Oh, no," reassured the doctor. "She would only go there during the day for her therapy sessions. And you can be with her if you want, though they also have a respite area onsite where you can sit and rest. You can even watch your daughter on a closed-circuit television from that room, though from what I hear, many parents relax so completely for the first time in years that sometimes they even fall asleep while their children are working with the therapists. And then, after every session, Aurora would come back home with you, of course. Does this sound like something you might want to try?"

José and Sophia looked at one another. Even without words, they finally understood what the other person was thinking and feeling. They knew that none of what had happened to them was their own fault. They finally believed everything that the doctors had been telling them for years was true and that Aurora's premature birth was a fluke of nature. They also knew how much they loved their daughter and each other. And they knew the toll it was taking to be the only ones offering round-the-clock care to Aurora and they knew that if they continued on this current path, they couldn't guarantee how much longer they would be able to sustain the high level of required, persistent effort that was required. Aurora was growing older and bigger and soon it would be almost impossible to physically handle her. As much as they tried, they couldn't imagine her being prepared to attend let alone succeed in school without some kind of intervention, for time was marching on and the day she would have to manage without them continually being nearby was rapidly approaching. And if they could get that assistance right now, from someone who truly understood the needs of their daughter, wouldn't that be a gift from Heaven?

All those thoughts passed between them in a moment's time and without uttering a word, they smiled at each other, turned to face the doctor and nodded at the same time. Aurora stopped crying, Sophia's back pain eased a little, and José slowed down his toe tapping just a bit.

But then, just a moment later, José's face clouded over as he wondered if they could afford such therapy.

The doctor answered his unasked question, "Just to be clear, there will be no cost for this service. The place I am thinking of to send Aurora is a charitable mission. I've been out many times to visit with Sally and Mateo, who run The Palm Tree Ranch, and I'm always impressed with the progress of each of their clients."

José and Sophia both smiled upon hearing this wonderful news. And Aurora must have sensed the happy and positive vibes in the air in the air as she let out a gentle giggle.

José spoke for them all as he told the doctor, "Sign us up!"

The doctor smiled as well and said he would arrange an appointment for their first visit to The Palm Tree Ranch. "But one more thing I want you to be prepared for ... Aurora will probably be put up on the back of one of their horses on your very first visit. Might seem a bit unconventional, but believe me, this equine therapy really works. Please be open to it."

"Horses!" exclaimed Sophia. "I wasn't expecting that one! But I'm willing to try it. How about you, José?"

José closed his eyes as he let out a long sigh, hugged his daughter just a little bit tighter to his chest and calmly said, "Count me in! Please set it up, Doctor. And thank you."

And thus, it began. On their very first visit to The Palm Tree Ranch, that little child who still had trouble sitting up on her own was indeed lifted up and positioned upon the back of the noble Buttermilk.

Not left up there on her own, of course. Aurora was carefully held in place by Mateo on one side and Gabriel on the other. Rider and spotters moved in unison as Buttermilk began to slowly walk around the paddock. It was clear to everyone right at the outset that Aurora loved being up there, perched high in the saddle, for she immediately relaxed and thoroughly enjoyed the ride, short as it was for this first day of therapy because at that time, Aurora was only able to attend and sit still for a few minutes. But over the course of the next few months, her attention span greatly increased until she became able to stay up on Buttermilk for almost half an hour at a time.

Without being directed, Aurora figured out how to rock herself gently back and forth as the horse shifted weight from one side to the other, making the slow and deliberate walks around the large circle in the ring easier and easier for her to manage on her own. Of course, Mateo and Gabriel were always right there, standing on either side of Buttermilk, ready to support the little girl as required, but the need to hold on to her all the time lessened with each riding session and soon the two men were able to simply keep one hand each lightly on Aurora's back, spotting her instead of holding tightly onto her.

Sally also began focusing on joint attention development with Aurora in the on-site classroom that had been created at The Palm Tree Ranch. The original goal for Aurora was to foster the development of specific skills, getting her able to both attend to instructions and perform tasks at the same time (I heard someone once use the phrase "walk and chew gum" which kind of encapsulated the idea for me and I'm throwing it out there in case it does the same for you).

Aurora made an incredible amount of progress in a relatively short amount of time. All of those newly developed skills will surely serve her well as she heads off to school. At this rate of growth and development, it's clear she will be ready to participate in activities with her peers and will also be capable of absorbing the information that is being taught to her, as well.

Aurora's development at integrating skills became evident when she was not only able to remember the steps to groom a horse but was at ease independently doing so after a riding adventure.

Her parents never did take advantage of the respite room, as they loved standing outside the fenced arena, eyes glued on their beautiful daughter. During the in-class therapy sessions, they sat and watched behind the one-way mirror. I was not too surprised to witness this rapid change in Aurora's behaviors and abilities, as I had seen it happen countless times before, but I must say that I was shocked to see how quickly Sophia and José were healed. Boy oh boy, what a delight to see them both looking relaxed and well rested these days! And I can vouch for the accuracy of their reports that things at home have gotten easier and that they really appreciate having effective and specific therapeutic techniques they can incorporate into Aurora's daily life routine around the house.

Here we are, a year and a half after Aurora's first visit to The Palm Tree Ranch, and with each literal moment that passes, Aurora's development and growth are clearly evident on all sides, not only physically in how tall this young girl is becoming but also intellectually as she integrates various skills and abilities together and emotionally as she now smiles most of the time and giggles at the drop of a hat. And no, that one was not meant literally.

Sally nailed it at the outset when she predicted Aurora's potential. On the very first day that José and Sophia arrived at The Ranch with Aurora, she told the nervous parents not to expect overnight miracles but assured them that they would see a measure of improvement relatively quickly, summing it up by stating that "Small steps bring great change."

Now, looking back, it becomes obvious that everyone involved in Aurora's equine therapy plan took many small and consistent steps forward when developing and implementing her program. The critical reason that Aurora showed enormous progress so quickly was that there was a total alignment of goals for all involved. Time and again, Sally and Mateo have witnessed that when parents/guardians/caretakers, child, therapists, and horse all work together, a strong, bonded team gets formed. In Aurora's case, this bonded team bolstered them all and supported Aurora's development. The vision they held for Aurora's potential future served as their common goal and the belief in each other and in a higher power brought them the strength to move toward that vision.

Great progress has already been made but everyone is staying realistic. They know there is still quite a way to go to reach their final destination, which will be Aurora attending and succeeding in school, then making wise and appropriate choices to achieve her independence as she eventually enters adulthood.

The love, support, faith and determination now coming from those who work with Aurora are combining to become a series of unending blessings for everyone involved in her therapy. I, who am privileged to get glimpses into the future, can assure you that even greater progress will be made and Aurora's life will reach out and touch so many people in so many positive ways. Already, her parents are so much more relaxed and at ease; they now have the time and energy to revel in having the family they always dreamed about, though they are somewhat surprised and delighted as their family has extended beyond just the three of them to include all the members of The Palm Tree Ranch, humans and horses alike! And believe me when I tell you that even more wonderful things will happen as Aurora continues to regularly attend regular equine therapy sessions.

Aurora's future is bright, indeed!

Maria: On the Trail

Not all the children who come to The Palm Tree Ranch have parents there to support them or even have parents at home who (at best) ignore them.

Some are orphans.

With three of their own children between them and multiple foster children for whom they have taken into their home over the years, Sally and Mateo well know the power that caring and loving parenting has on the positive development of a child. Their house isn't big enough to bring in all the orphaned children in need, but they have found a way to offer their services to young people who all too often can get overlooked in a system of state-sponsored care: they linked up with the local orphanage and established a program to offer equine therapy to children in need who were charges of the state. And by need, Sally and Mateo primarily meant those children manifestly causing pain or suffering to others, those who hope that such overtly negative behaviors could somehow ameliorate their own suffering borne from years of abuse or abandonment.

Once the program was announced and made available, the names of several children living at the orphanage in town immediately rose to the top of the pile, but no child displayed more angry and needy behavior than a twelve-year-old girl named Maria. Relatively tall for her age, she tended to use her size against her peers, seeking out and persecuting those children who were smaller, younger or generally more vulnerable. Very quickly upon her arrival to the orphanage at the age of six, she developed a reputation for being a "difficult" child.

She tended not to listen to adults, was disruptive during class time in school, and regularly had severe meltdowns. In addition, she exhibited such personally unsafe behaviors as disappearing or hiding and had even made several attempts to run away.

The lifestyle Maria was leading did not seem surprising when held up against the backdrop of having to be placed in an orphanage as a result of her parents both dying within a few weeks of each other: first her mother of a drug overdose and then her father, who was shot by a police officer during an attempted bank robbery.

Though she never talked about it, records showed that Maria's upbringing was particularly violent and since coming to the orphanage she herself carried on that same pattern of violence toward others. With seemingly no provocation she would resort to physically fighting other children. Maria quickly became a menace to all the other young wards, most especially taking advantage of them whenever they were left unsupervised, even if only for a moment.

Her behaviors escalated with the passage of time until finally it became clear that Maria's anger held no boundaries and that she could and would hurt anyone who crossed her path. She railed not only against those who were her own age but also showed no fear in targeting those who were much older, as well. Verbal taunts and threats towards others were a way of life for Maria, who endangered the well-being of the children living around her and also caused concern for the personal safety of her adult guardians.

The director of the orphanage put forward a request to send Maria to equine therapy sessions at The Palm Tree Ranch and spoke with Sally and Mateo several times before they all agreed that going to The Ranch might well help Maria. And, at the very least, they knew it wouldn't hurt her. She was a child desperately crying out for help. Thankfully, Sally and Mateo heard and answered that cry.

It was decided to begin the sessions as soon as possible in hopes of preventing what would have to be the next step in the process if her violent tendencies went unchecked which would be sending Maria to a more closely guarded, secluded place of residence.

That following Monday, the car bringing Maria to The Ranch pulled up the pathway and stopped in front of where Sally was waiting. An older woman was driving the car and a large man was sitting next to a girl who was slouching in the rear seat. The man leaned forward a bit, pointed at Maria and spoke through the open window to Sally, "This one is a real handful. I'm warning you to be very careful. Don't turn your back on her. She won't hesitate to try to hurt you. Believe it or not, she even attacked the director over the weekend!"

Maria let out a huge moan, turned her head away from where Sally was standing to look out the front of the car and said out loud to no one in particular, "What kind of place is this, anyhow? It sure doesn't look like that other place where that stupid doctor makes me sit and talk to him. And it sure doesn't look like another stinking orphanage."

Maria obviously thought she was either being brought to meet with yet another psychologist or was going to the state-run child protective services known as DIF (Desarrollo de la integral Familia in Spanish—which translates to Development of the Integral Family in English) to be placed in the more secure shelter that was held over her head as a threat every time she displayed any kind of violent behavior.

"You are at The Palm Tree Ranch, Maria," Sally told the girl in a calm, even tone. She crouched down so that her face was visible through the open car window and continued talking, "My name is Sally and I will be here every time you come to visit. I know you've been having a really hard time since your mother and father died a few years ago. I'm so sorry about everything you've gone through, but we all want you to help you find more positive ways to deal with life in general and more specifically, with the people around you."

As Sally began speaking, Maria turned her head and, with a face devoid of emotions, stared directly into Sally's eyes. Sally had the strangest feeling that Maria was looking through instead of at her.

Once Sally finished talking, Maria held her gaze for a minute, then turned her head so she once again was looking out toward the front of the car. Another few moments of silence went by before Maria asked out loud, once again talking to no one in particular, "Ranch? Why did I get brought to a ranch?"

"You're here to meet and spend time with the best workers we have here … our horses!"

As soon as she heard what Sally said, Maria quickly sat up in her seat but continued to look straight ahead toward the front window of the car. She said nothing but, for the first time since she had arrived, emotion showed on her face, quickly running the gamut from shock, to fear, to confusion, and finally to apprehension, one right after the other in rapid succession.

Maria blinked a few times, shook her head back and forth very quickly as if trying to wake herself from a dream. It was then that she turned her attention out the other car window, which was when she saw them. Not one or two, but all four horses wandering around in the nearby fenced-in paddock. Sometimes on outings from the orphanage, Maria had seen horses out being ridden in the fields or grazing in the meadows as the vehicle quickly drove down the road, but she never had time to really take in all that she was seeing and certainly had never gotten up this close to look at a herd of horses all gathered together. Now here she was, looking at these animals who were only a few paces away from the car. Deep down, Maria felt like she should still be angry about being brought here to this place without even being asked, but instead her mind closed off to anger or any other negative feelings because she was completely overtaken by staring at the beautiful animals standing so close to her.

Those horses were so much bigger than she ever could have imagined but amazingly, they didn't frighten her at all. Just the opposite. Something about them made her feel calm inside. The gamut of expressions continued until her facial muscles finally settled down and remained on the one that indicated curiosity. Maria said nothing, but slid over the car seat so she could reach the door handle. She pushed it down and bumped the door open with her shoulder. She got out of the car and looked around. The only one standing there was that lady who said her name was Sally. There were no other adults or children in sight.

Maria moved a bit away from the car and as soon as the driver saw this, she put the automobile into gear and quickly headed away, calling out that they would return in an hour to pick Maria up and bring her back to the orphanage.

And there the two of them stood, Maria looking at the horses and Sally looking at Maria. Over the past weekend, Sally and Mateo had developed a clear plan of action for their first meeting with the young girl. They knew they had to gain her confidence and they also needed some time to evaluate her. Best for Sally and Maria to begin alone together, separated from the others on the property. But little did Maria realize, though, that she and Sally were not really all alone, for both Mateo and Gabriel were working just out of sight nearby in the barn, ready and willing to help out in case Sally called for assistance should a physical altercation arise.

Maria wasn't looking for a fight, though. She planted her feet firmly on the ground and just stood there, keeping watch on the herd from afar. She let her gaze shift from one horse to another, taking in the sights, sounds and smells of being this near these amazing animals.

As for the horses, they mostly ignored this new visitor and instead quietly continued to graze on the grass at their feet.

Sally kept looking at the young girl and the two of them stayed silent for quite a while. And then, ever so slowly, Sally walked to the fence to peer over the rails at the horses. Maria followed and also stood at the railing, making sure to keep her distance from Sally. The young girl's eyes stayed firmly planted forward, providing her with a clear view of the four horses wandering out there in the paddock.

"What do you think of them?" Sally finally asked.

Maria just kept looking at the horses, totally captivated by their size and beauty. She said nothing, but it was obvious how she was feeling, because for the first time since she arrived at The Ranch, she was smiling.

Sally went on talking as if Maria had responded, "I think they are all so beautiful, each in their own right. For now, you get to observe our herd so you can become familiar with their ways. And then you will come to see that they each have such different personalities! These four particular horses are very special animals because, one and all, they are patient with new people and they really like to take children for rides. But before you get to ride them, you have to get to know them. And to do that, you will need to learn how to take care of them and prove that you will be calm and gentle around them. Of course, this will require some time, but trust me, it will be worth it, for one day you will get up on the back of one of these wonderful animals and you and I will go for a ride down that trail over there."

Maria looked down the trail and then turned to face Sally, then looked down the trail once again.

"I think I might like it here," she said quietly, almost to herself.

And that very moment, so seemingly unremarkable, became the turning point for Maria's whole life.

From that day on, Maria practically jumped in the backseat of the car when the orphanage driver told her it was time to head to The Palm Tree Ranch. After the first few times of this routine, it was decided that they no longer needed a guard to sit next to Maria on the drives to The Ranch, as she no longer posed a threat to the driver. Maria would sit quietly in the back seat, staring out the window, eagerly awaiting the final turn of their journey where they would pass the sign that told them they had arrived at The Palm Tree Ranch. So excited to be there, she would hardly wait for the automobile to stop before pushing open her door and running over to the paddock fence.

Maria carefully listened to Sally as the secrets of horses were revealed. She learned all about the nature of those animals in general, about herd behavior and the way that they communicate both with each other and with humans. She was shown how to take care of them so they stayed healthy and happy. Most of all, Maria enjoyed hearing the life stories of each of the four horses and often asked Sally (and later Mateo or Gabriel) to tell her how they all came to be living and working at The Palm Tree Ranch.

Over time, Maria was encouraged to learn how to groom the horses. She followed these directions to the letter, making sure that she did exactly as she had been taught. All the grooming materials for each horse were gathered into their own individual wooden containers and Maria was always careful to choose the caddy designated for the specific horse being groomed. Once that horse was secured in the stall with a quick release knot on the rope, she would walk over, pick up each leg in turn to inspect the hooves and with her hands gently remove any rocks or big clumps of dirt embedded in the shoes. Then, with a somewhat stiff curry comb, she would rub all over the horse's coat in a circular motion to loosen any embedded particles such as dirt or dead hair. She knew the horses liked currying because it felt to them almost like getting a massage. She took her time brushing each side of the horse's body, from the neck to the barrel to the rump.

She never worried if the horse wiggled its nose or even nipped at her while she was brushing it because she knew that this was just the horse's way of trying to return the favor for the comforting treatment. When it happened, she would laugh and gently push the horse's nose away, saying, "I don't need grooming today, thank you very much."

When she was done bringing up all the embedded dirt and hair on the horse's body, she would switch to a dandy brush so she could remove the debris for once and for all. She did this by using long sweeping strokes downward and away from the horse. Maria enjoyed this part because she knew this particular brushing technique not only ensured that the horse's body was all cleaned off but it also helped the horse feel soothed and relaxed, as well.

Next, she would very carefully clean the horse's face, first with a very soft brush and then with a dampened sponge. When that was done, she got a different wet sponge so she could clean the dock area under the tail. And finally, using a wide-bristled comb, she would brush the mane and tail.

It took time and patience to groom a horse, but Maria never complained. In fact, she looked forward to the opportunity to take care of each horse in the herd and was always the first to volunteer to groom any horse that needed it.

Maria never rushed the grooming procedure. And the horses never got antsy or exhibited any impatience while being groomed by her. In a slow-paced, methodical fashion, one type of cleaning followed the next and the horse would go from looking dirty to sparkling clean. Each time, when she completed the whole procedure, Maria would stand back and with much pride in her voice, give the recipient of her efforts the exact same praise, "Now, don't you look lovely! Your coat is shiny and I swear that it downright glistens!"

Grooming was not all that Maria learned during her time at The Palm Tree Ranch. It was only a few weeks into her therapy program that, with lots of help, she was able to put the halter on the horse so she and Sally could lead them around the ring, one after another, each in turn.

Seeing how careful Maria was while walking with the different horses, Sally knew it was time for another big step in her equine therapy program.

When Maria arrived on the next sunny morning, jumping out of the car and running over to the paddock fence as usual, Sally greeted her by saying, "Let's take a moment before we start working with the horses today. Let's just stand and watch as they mingle together. You've met them all, you've worked with them and you've groomed each one.

Now, as you look at them, tell me what you notice about each of these horses in this herd."

Maria paused and looked around her, taking in the sights and sounds of the four beautiful animals grazing out there in the field. Finally, she inhaled a deep breath, let it out, and said, "Well, I see that there is a group of three that really stick together and then there is Henry, who is kinda out doing his own thing."

Sally nodded and agreed with Maria. Then she asked the girl, "Of these four horses, which one do you think is most like yourself?"

Maria laughed and quickly responded, "That's an easy one! It's Henry. Look at him. Near the group but really out there all on his own. That's how I feel most of the time. Kinda isolated." She thought for a moment and then continued, "You know something? Even though I'm with all those other kids at the orphanage, they do their thing and I do mine. I don't need to be close friends with them. I kinda like being independent. And you know what's really funny? I just realized the other day that I sure don't need to bully them like I used to do."

Maria paused, nodded a few times to herself before adding, "Yeah. Nowadays we just go our separate ways at the orphanage and I like it like that. And Henry does that same thing here with these other horses."

"Well then," Sally said, "Go on over and get Henry. Put the halter on him and walk him around the arena."

Maria looked momentarily terrified and asked Sally, "You mean do that all by myself?"

Sally nodded. "You're ready and Henry will love working with you because he will sense that the two of you are soulmates. And I'll tell you a little secret ... even though you both like to be alone, sometimes it's nice to have a friend around. Go be Henry's friend."

Sally promised to stay in the arena but said she would stand just a bit away from Maria. Sally reassured the girl that she would remain nearby so she could easily step in to help with Henry just in case anything unexpected or worrisome happened. Maria nodded and whispered to herself as the gate opened and she walked through, "I can do this. I can do this. I can do this."

And she did.

Later at dinner that night, well after Maria had left The Palm Tree Ranch, Sally and Mateo were discussing how important it was to develop a sense of trust in these children with whom they worked. The two of them agreed that, even though it was essential, it was not always easy.

They remarked about how when Maria first arrived at The Ranch many months ago, it was clear she didn't trust anything or anyone. So, being willing and able to deal with Henry earlier that day, even though it was initially hard for Maria, turned out just as they had hoped it would and when they saw her leading him around the paddock all by herself, they knew that this new activity certainly helped to further develop the bond of trust between the young girl and the horse.

During the next few sessions, Maria became comfortable taking care of Henry entirely on her own without even asking for any help or support, so Sally opted to stand outside the fence instead of staying inside the arena. Maria happily spent time walking Henry around and quietly talked to him the whole time. Whenever she looked up and saw Sally, Maria would break out into a huge grin and always appeared very proud of herself.

One day, after Maria and Henry had walked together for a while, Sally had her bring the horse to the far side of the arena to be groomed. During the grooming, Maria stopped brushing for a moment and told Sally that she needed help cleaning Henry's hooves. Sally asked why and was totally surprised when Maria hesitated before explaining, "I never used the hoof pick before. I've always just cleaned the shoes out by hand. It's time I learned how to do it right. But I'm afraid I might hurt him and I really don't want to hurt him."

Sally was surprised to hear what Maria said.

And quite honestly, I myself was surprised as well. Even though I am able to read the thoughts of the horses and to understand the feelings of the children who come to The Palm Tree Ranch, I wasn't prepared for this caring and considerate side of Maria to emerge so quickly and so strongly, and I surely never anticipated that she would be able to express her thoughts in such a clear-cut manner. Before Maria first came to The Ranch, she would lash out and hurt all those who tried to get near her. Now here she was, worried about causing pain to another living being. Working and bonding with Henry was helping to give Maria some insight and understanding that her actions had consequences, not only for herself but for others. Amazing progress was being made, to say the least!

Sally resisted the urge to sweep Maria up in her arms and give her a big hug, because she knew Maria tended to shy away from any physical contact, and even such a loving and innocent gesture as an unexpected hug might very well upset the young girl. Instead, Sally kept her distance, nodded and said, "No problem. I'll show you how to do it so Henry's hooves get cleaned without hurting him at all. But when we're done, be ready because he is probably going to try to nuzzle you. Remember, that's his way of saying thank you. You already know that he really enjoys getting groomed but you're about to find out that most especially he likes to have his hooves cleaned!"

And what Sally predicted was exactly what happened. Surprisingly, this time Maria not only accepted the nuzzling from Henry but she reached her arms around his neck and gave him a hug in return. It was the first hug Maria ever offered anyone in many years and that action helped Sally see that this therapy plan was on the right track. All her life Maria had been, of necessity, very protective of herself. Over the years, she learned that her most reliable defense mechanism was to lash out in anger and be violent with others. But here she was, now, for the first time ever, finally able to relax a bit and to reach out to show how she felt when she was happy.

The next time that Maria came to visit, as she got out of the car and raced over to the paddock, Henry looked over at her then dropped his head, pointed his ears toward the front of his body, and began to lick and chew, even though there was no food in his mouth.

"What's wrong with Henry?" Maria asked to no one in particular. "I never saw him acting so weird. Oh my gosh, I hope he's not sick"

Mateo had just come out of the barn, heard what Maria had said, laughed and told her, "Sick with love maybe."

Sally joined them and said, "Mateo is teasing you. Don't worry. Henry is fine. He's just letting us know that he's looking forward to working with you today. The way Henry is behaving right now lets us know that he trusts you and is confident that you won't hurt him."

Maria's jaw dropped open and she looked away while trying to take this information in, then finally looked back at Henry and said to him, "You trust me. You trust me not to hurt you. Well, Henry, you're right! I never would do anything to hurt you. Never, ever, ever."

"That's great to hear, Maria," Sally told the young girl. "And it's great that Henry trusts you. Now the question is, do you trust him?"

"Oh yes!"

"Then since you aren't a horse and can't make your ears point forward, let's figure out another way that you can let him know that you trust him."

Maria laughed and said, "Yeah, let's. But I don't have any ideas how to do it. How do people let horses know they trust them?"

"Simple. It's time for you to get up on Henry's back and ride him around the ring. "

"Wow. I thought this day would never come! Should we put his saddle on him?"

Sally shook her head and said, "No. Not yet. You can start by riding Henry bare back. I'll stay with you. All you have to do is relax and figure out how to find your balance."

Sally held onto the halter the whole time that Henry walked around the arena. She calmly kept reminding Maria that Henry would never hurt her, that he would always be gentle with her because he understood that was exactly what she needed during their time riding together.

After the therapy session ended and Maria started to get into the car to head back to the orphanage, she stopped for a moment, turned and said to Sally, "This was the best day ever! I loved riding with Henry!"

"Oh, that's great to hear," responded Sally. "Today was the first time you rode Henry, but it sure won't be your last. He'll be waiting for you next time you come and I know he will be looking forward to riding with you."

Over time, Maria became more and more comfortable sitting up on Henry's back. Sally suggested that when Maria rode with Henry, she could try several different exercises to further strengthen the trust between rider and horse, so she had Maria sit sideways, backwards, and then return to facing forward; she had her lie down completely on Henry's back to give him a big hug around his neck; and finally she even temporarily put a blindfold around Maria's eyes to give her a chance not to think about where they were going but instead to focus on what it felt like to sit atop a strong horse as it moved slowly and gently forward. Maria enjoyed all of those exercises and became a stronger, more confident rider because of them. And finally, Maria learned how to put the saddle on Henry so she could ride him that way, too.

One day, while Maria was riding around the ring, Sally was watching from afar. Then she unlatched the gate and walked into the arena, coming over to greet the horse and rider. Sally reached out and took Henry's reins, running her hands along his mane while she spoke directly to Maria, telling her, "I have some wonderful news for you. It's clear to me that you and Henry are now best friends for life. From this point forward, every time you come to visit and ride together, you can take him down the trail away from everyone else. This way you can tell Henry any and every single thing you want. You can share all the good, fabulous, bad, horrible or sad thoughts and memories you have inside of you. Henry will listen to you and amazingly, he will understand it all. And this is the best part: he will never tell a soul! You can put all your trust in him. When you ride together, Henry will carry you on his shoulders and for now and always, he'll be there for you, ready to support you however you need."

Maria did not respond directly to Sally, but instead she laid her head down on Henry's neck, held onto him and cried. Her tears were a combination of sadness over knowing all the terrible and tragic stories from her life that she kept hidden deep down inside and joy that she now had someone with whom she could share them all.

Now, even though I am not permitted to directly interfere with relationships between life forces here on this planet, I myself wonder how it happens that sometimes the stars seem to align and several good things all happen at once. One such example of this confluence of positive energy took place on that very day, for instead of the regular driver, the director of the orphanage just happened to have brought Maria to The Palm Tree Ranch. And instead of heading off like the regular driver always did, the director decided to stay and observe the therapy session firsthand. Sitting on the porch of the ranch house, she became privy to witnessing this emotional scene.

As she saw Maria begin to cry, the director turned to Mateo who was sitting next to her and said, "I can't believe this is the same girl we brought here only a few months ago! All those years we spent trying to help her to not to overreact when things didn't go her way and to not be violent toward others. We tried for so long, but we never had success. Things just seemed to get worse. But here at The Ranch, you and Sally made a remarkably positive breakthrough with her!"

Mateo sat quietly for a moment before answering, then said, "Yes, we helped. But really most of the credit for all of this goes to that stocky red dun-colored horse over there. Henry Street or just plain Henry as we call him. He is truly our miracle worker in this case."

And what Mateo said proved to be true, for after that day, each time when Maria came to ride, she would put on the saddle, hoist herself up on Henry's back and as the two of them headed out over the trails together, she would talk and talk, quietly telling him all about her hurts, her worries, her painful memories, her fears, her doubts, as well as her dreams and her hopes for a better life. And Henry not only carried Maria on his shoulders, as Sally had said he would, but he carried all of that which she shared with him. Hearing what she said made Henry stand just a bit taller and stronger, almost as if he was making sure Maria felt safe and loved.

Now, I don't want you to get the idea that life is perfect for Maria. She still lives in the orphanage and probably will until she ages out of the system and is forced to go find her way on her own. And she still has her ups and downs in dealing with her feelings of anger and frustration, but from that first day of being with the horses, she has tried her best to find ways other than violence to solve her problems. She is now remorseful when she does not listen to the caregivers at the orphanage. She apologizes after she loses her temper. And most importantly, she has not hit or hurt another person since she started coming to The Palm Tree Ranch.

In fact, since she started working with Henry, she has even has taken to offering hugs to fellow students and caregivers at the orphanage when something wonderful happens or when she thinks they could use a bit of friendly, loving care.

So, finally it happened. One day, when Maria arrived for her usual therapy session, instead of handing her a saddle, Sally and Mateo brought her over to the porch, telling her they wanted to sit and chat for a while. Maria got nervous, as it was clear something different was about to happen, but she went over and sat down, quietly sipping on the glass of lemonade that was poured for her.

Sally began by saying, "We have some good news and then some even better news for you." Before Maria could respond, Sally went on to explain, "First of all, you've made such amazing progress since first arriving here at The Ranch that it's clear we should be ending your therapeutic riding sessions. You don't need them anymore and we need to make space in our schedule for other children who need our services far more than you do."

Maria's eyes welled with tears and she spoke with a choked voice as she said, "How can you say that's good news? Never to get to ride on Henry again? It can't be true! Please! No!"

Sally reached out to comfort Maria, patted her arm and said, "Oh, believe me, it really is good news, Maria! You've changed so much during since you've been coming here. We are so proud of you. Honestly, you don't need regular therapy sessions anymore."

Maria tried to think about what she should say, but knew she needed some time before speaking, so she picked up her glass and gulped down some lemonade.

Sally spoke instead. "Maria, remember I said there was good news and then even better news. And you haven't heard the even better news yet."

Maria turned and looked at directly at Sally, trying to imagine what that news would be.

"We would love for you to still come to The Ranch just as regularly as you have been doing. But instead of us helping you, we would like for you to volunteer to help other children. And while you're here on those visits, Henry will be waiting patiently for you when you finish your work so the two of you can go riding together!"

Maria's mouth dropped open. Her eyes grew wide. She blinked several times before shouting, "Yes! Yes! Of course, yes!"

Maria now comes to The Palm Tree Ranch every week. She willingly does everything asked of her and sometimes has called upon her own background, experiences, skills and abilities to suggest an idea that would help a child gain trust and confidence with a particular horse.

Maria can often be seen walking or running beside the horses as they carry the children, offering support by spotting them while they ride and sometimes will double-mount ride with a child who does not have the physical strength to sit on the horse alone, holding onto the child perched in front of her so the two of them can ride together. She is, without exception, patient and tender during all of these directed therapy sessions and easily bonds with each and every child with whom she works, almost as if both of them instinctively understand where they have been and share a vision of where they could be going.

Sally and Mateo have been a large part of this journey and have loved seeing how Maria shifted from being a child in need to one who cares for others in need. In fact, because they were so impressed with Maria's ability to connect with the children during their therapy sessions, they began discussing the idea of hiring her as a full-time ranch hand once she graduated from school.

When Gabriel was brought in on the talks, he was totally supportive of the idea and said that Maria would make a perfect ranch hand, as he was most impressed with the person she had become and knew that her strong work ethic would not only serve her well but also be great for all the other workers.

For now, though, Maria continues to go to school and to volunteer at The Palm Tree Ranch on a regular basis. She is always the first to offer comforting words when the going is tough and never ceases to be thrilled when the children make strides in their therapy plans.

And when Sally and Maria stop and remember way back to when Maria finished her own therapy sessions, they both talk about the "even better news" that Sally had mentioned then. Now, week after week, as Maria finishes her volunteer work, she always takes a deep breath, looks all around her, then calmly walks over to where Henry is standing, patiently waiting. Maria saddles him up and the two of them ride off on the path down into the far fields, sometimes at a running pace but mostly just walking slowly so Maria can easily lean down and whisper in Henry's ear, sharing all her thoughts and dreams, just like always.

Shared Blessings

Such a joyful journey my time of existence is taking me on! Coming from so far away and across multiple galaxies, always observing the comings and goings of things around me and then, finally winding up here on this particular planet.

Although my main assignment has been to hover above, next to, and near, always in the background like a shadow, how thoroughly grateful I am when I've been given permission to occasionally offer whispers of ideas and provide a path to insights. Over all the years I have been on duty here on Earth, witnessing the changes and developments that have occurred, well, it boggles the mind, to say the least!

Of all the assignments I have ever received, I often tell The One Who Guides Us All that being here on this planet is my favorite. What a joyful blessing it is to have this opportunity to watch over and gently guide all who live here—the plants, the animals and most especially, the humans.

Centuries of floating around those who live on this orb has finally led me to this most recent and blessed task: to watch over those living and working at The Palm Tree Ranch.

Even though time is a concept that is relatively meaningless to me and others of my ilk, I know it is important to the people living here on Earth. So, as I am now attuned to the ticking of the clocks all around me, I note that I have seen minutes turn into hours, which have turned into days, weeks, months and years. During all the time I've spent at The Ranch, so many children have been served by the knowledge, skills and love that Sally and Mateo bring to this mission. Through each of the physical therapy sessions and even more importantly through each of the equine therapy sessions, those children being served have grown and developed into the best, strongest versions of themselves.

The One Who Guides Us All recently called upon me to come and visit. During the time we spent together, The One kindly told me, "Thou-Est, I am so very proud of you. I have observed how much you have progressed and evolved during each of your various assignments, with none more powerful as what has been done in this latest project."

"Thank you so much, I never expected to receive such high praise from you" I humbly responded. But then a worrisome thought crossed my mind and so I asked, "Are you changing my assignment? Will I need to be leaving The Ranch?"

"Oh, no, not at all. In fact, your assignment there will continue as long as The Palm Tree Ranch stays in existence. Their work is very important to so many. It would be wrong to leave them with no direct spiritual support."

I nodded and said, "Yes, of course. Why, when I think about all those children who have had therapy there, I can't help but be amazed at the goodness that has happened on The Palm Tree Ranch!"

The One agreed with me, though went on to add, "You are right. The most important part of this mission is the children, but surely you can see that the ripples of positive goodness reach so much farther than merely to those children themselves. Think also of all the parents, guardians and caretakers whose worries have been lifted and how their fears have been assuaged."

Once again, I nodded in agreement.

The One continued, "Now think about all the ranch hands who work so hard to take care of the horses and make sure the outbuildings, the homestead, the barn, the arena, the paddock and the trails are all maintained. They don't just do this work for the paychecks they receive but they also do it out of love and appreciation for the mission of The

Ranch. On top of that, there are also so many volunteers who come on a regular basis to help maintain the tools, to clean out the stables and to serve as spotters for children when they ride on the horses. Oh, and think about all those people who believe in the mission but have never been to The Palm Tree Ranch—the financial support of their monetary donations enables Sally and Mateo to accomplish all this work without every charging anyone, which means all those in need are welcomed and served."

"So wide is the net of goodness!" I exclaimed. "Lately I've been focused so much on the children that I've overlooked all those other people."

The One paused for a moment, perhaps giving me time to mull over what I had just said. That one moment was all it took for an ah-ha on my part, as I added, "But it hasn't been only people who have benefitted from the work being done at The Ranch!"

"Go on," encouraged The One.

"It's been the horses in the herd, too."

"Yes, yes, yes! And anyone or anything else?"

I looked back in my mind to review all that had happened at The Palm Tree Ranch since I first arrived. Scenes of the early days when Sally and Mateo found the place, with dirt and mud covering everything, with the barn roof falling down, with the house in filthy disarray and with the trails wildly overgrown sifted ever so slowly through my mind and through time until now, with grass growing in the fenced-in areas, with dry flooring in the barn, individual stalls built and a sturdy roof installed above, with the main house cleaned and organized, with a shed designed and constructed for storage and with a ranch house where the workers could live on the property if they so choose, and with all the trails carefully manicured and well-used.

Before I could verbalize my thoughts, The One read my mind and said, "You are right. So much in the surrounding environment, all those things living and even those things that have been created by people, have profited from the care and attention of Sally and Mateo in their capacity as directors of The Palm Tree Ranch."

Feelings of contentment and joy washed over me. In turn, those blessings moved outward in waves that extended far, far into the Universe.

Good begets good.

And as our meeting was coming to an end, I began to say a fond farewell but The One held me back a moment to remind me that even though I was returning to Earth and to The Palm Tree Ranch, distance and time actually held a different meaning to us.

"True," I said. "Though far from each other, we are but a thought and a prayer away."

"And even though some people on Earth may not realize it, the same as it is for us, the same it is for all of them walking around on that beautiful planet," said The One.

With that, there was nothing more needing to be said, so I headed back to my assigned place, hovering around and near those at The Palm Tree Ranch.

I have been given the honor of watching over everything that occurs at The Ranch. But those who also serve—including Sally, Mateo, Gabriel, Maria and all the other ranch hands and volunteers—do so more directly, though none the less purposefully than all of us who come from the Heavens above.

One purpose.

One mission.

We are bonded together with this shared vision: to strengthen and positively alter the lives of selected children who, for one reason or another, started off on a somewhat uneven playing field. To give those children assistance through learning techniques and specific strategies so they not only survive but they also thrive as they make their way through the rest of their days on Earth.

As a result of this mission, the horses themselves, who were once neglected and dismissed have now found peace and contentment, filled with joy in the knowledge that their interactions with the children who come to The Palm Tree Ranch have made things better for everyone involved. Sally and Mateo continue putting forth maximum effort every single day, working hard but never minding. The confidence they feel in their shared purpose for living bolsters the love they have for each other, which only grows stronger with each moment that passes. The Palm Tree Ranch, as it continues to thrive, is making their dreams come true and consequently the dreams of all those whose lives they touch.

Yes indeed ... Good begets good.

About the Author

While Jean T. Slobodzian now holds the title of Professor Emeritus at The College of New Jersey, she began her career teaching elementary and secondary students in a variety of locations across the United States. She also served as a nationally certified English-American Sign Language interpreter during that same time.

Now happily retired, she has made the shift from scholarly academic writing to creating works of fiction and poetry, and has begun the journey of recounting her own life events in memoir form.